MISADVENTURES

WITH A

PROFESSOR

BY
SIERRA SIMONE

MISADVENTURES

WITH A

PROFESSOR

BY
SIERRA SIMONE

WATERHOUSE PRESS

To Ashley Brown Morris and Kate Fasse—
Our friendship uses only the good notes.

CHAPTER ONE

ZANDY

I forgot the umbrella.

I remembered a backup battery charger, lipstick, condoms, my passport, a disposable toothbrush, and an appropriate amount of petty cash in case of emergency. I spent hours perfecting my hair and makeup into a look that proclaimed the perfect blend of sexual and social experience. I researched my route and destination and reviewed my notes for the plan.

I was prepared for every single contingency—except the most obvious one, which is that it rains in England sometimes.

Okay, a lot of times. It rains in England *a lot of times.*

And I forgot the damn umbrella in my hotel room.

I squint up at the street sign on the building next to me and then back down to my phone, trying to get my bearings. Unfortunately, the rain has made it nearly impossible to view the app on my screen, and even more unfortunately, I'm certain I've never come across this street in all my planning and preparation, which means I'm definitely lost—although it's hard to tell, given how London streets rename themselves at bafflingly random intervals.

And it's while I'm standing there trying to rub my rain-spattered screen on my equally rain-spattered dress that the silver drizzle decides to become a downpour, darkening the already dim evening and soaking through my dress and hair in a matter of seconds.

"Shit!" I mutter, cupping a hand over my eyes, trying to peer through the chilling curtain of rain. I can't even see across the street, much less try to get my bearings.

"Shit, shit, shit."

A black cab hisses by, sending a wave of water up and over my only pair of high heels—bought specially for tonight and the plan—and it's the last straw. Screw getting my bearings. I want to get *dry*. I start walking, heels *squelch-squelching* as I go, and in a fit of pique, I yank them off my feet and start jogging barefoot down the slick sidewalk, wondering how my perfectly orchestrated agenda got so off-kilter.

When my father arranged for me to spend the summer with an old friend of his as a research assistant, I was beyond excited. An entire summer in the English countryside cataloging old books and annotating metadata? Basically paradise for me.

But my real excitement came when I realized I'd have a night alone in London before I went to Professor Graeme's house. A single night in one of the best cities in the world to fix a very serious problem of mine:

I, Zandy Lynch, twenty-two years old and soon-to-be-graduate student, am a virgin. And that is no longer acceptable.

I'm tired of ending my nights with a skinny margarita and a vibrator. I'm tired of dates that go nowhere, tired of coming home alone, tired of lying in bed with a hollow *ache* that no amount of battery power can massage away. And it was as I was poring over my acceptance letter for library school that I realized I've become that silly old stereotype: the spinster librarian. The virgin nerd.

Ugh.

It's not *fair*. I never asked to be a virgin at twenty-two! I never asked to be a spinster! All I ever asked for was a cute guy with a willing penis.

Okay, well, and a college education—preferably graduate level or higher.

And a good job—preferably in academia or a related field.

And an extensive shared list of common interests—including, but not limited to, modern literature, premodern literature, postmodern literature, Tolkien marginalia, crossword puzzles, animals, coffee, travel to places where druids sacrificed virgins, and variations of fruit pie.

So maybe my standards were a little high.

I started the plan the way I start everything—with a trip to the library. I outlined my objectives, decided on my research methodology, and created a timeline. I devoured books, articles, studies, and anecdotal data about how to get over my hymen-hurdle, and after all that, I came to a very certain conclusion.

I'd been going about this all wrong.

Sex is supposed to be spontaneous, unforced, mutually initiated. I can't plan my way into someone's pants...but I *can* plan the perfect environment to facilitate depantsing. So when Dad surprised me with the research vacation, I knew this night in London was my chance to find the perfect depantsing environment.

Except now it's raining and I'm lost and barefoot and the plan has quickly unraveled into a wet, chilly disaster.

Okay, Zandy, focus.

There was a tube station marked on my phone's map before the water made it totally impossible to navigate—maybe it's just past the next cross street? I'll duck inside, out of the rain, get my phone working again, and think of my next steps. And check my makeup.

I only have tonight, after all, and I'm not ready to give up, umbrella or not.

I pick up my jog, my head bent down to shield my eyes from the worst of the rain, the sopping-wet hem of my dress slapping and sticking around my thighs, when I collide with a firm chest and wheeze out an *oof.* Something resembling a grunt comes from the chest.

From him.

Warm hands come up to my elbows to steady me, and I look up into a pale face marked by darkly slashed eyebrows, high cheekbones, and a squared, clean-shaven jaw. His eyes in the rainy night seem like every kind of color, light and dark, brown and blue and green, and they're framed by the longest, sultriest lashes I've ever seen on a man.

But it's his mouth that fascinates me—slightly too wide and slightly too thin but hauntingly pretty, with perfectly formed peaks at his upper lip and a tantalizing hint of fullness to his lower one. Rain drips from his cheeks and the longish ends of his dark hair to catch along the sharp edges of his lips and gather in the tempting bow of his philtrum.

And with a sudden illicit thrill, I realize I want to lick the rainwater off those lips. I want to kiss them until they're warm and soft under my own. I want to feel the shape of his mouth under mine, murmuring my name—except...

That perfect, rain-slicked mouth is currently creased in a harsh, unhappy scowl.

CHAPTER TWO

OLIVER

She's shivering.

It takes me a moment to notice, as I'm still processing how someone emerged out of this tempest right in front of me. I'm also still processing how this someone in question is a creature made of pale skin, dark hair, and a sinfully red and lush mouth. Like a vampiress straight from a storybook but with the most incongruously innocent eyes I've ever seen.

She's also young, drenched to the bone, and utterly, utterly inappropriately dressed for a night like this.

"Why aren't you wearing a coat?" I demand over the roar of the rain, and her gaze blinks up at me—which is when I realize she's been staring at my mouth. A kick of heat goes straight to my cock.

I ignore it.

"And why are you barefoot?"

Her eyes flick back to my frowning mouth, and her own mouth parts ever so slightly, as if my bad-tempered scowl fascinates her. Her tongue darts over her lower lip, licking away a bead of rainwater that settled over her fire-engine-red lipstick, and I find I want her to do it again. And again. And again.

I could watch her licking rain off her lips for the rest of my life.

"I'm looking for the Goose and Gander," she finally offers. It's hard to hear her over the rain, and yet even with the *whoosh* and *churr* of the torrent, I can hear her accent. Broad and wide and a little flat, American television style.

I know where the Goose and Gander is. I just came from there, actually, having endured a meal deconstructed into various mason jars and served on a wooden plank for the sake of seeing some old friends. But I'd drawn the line at overpriced cocktails decanted into chemistry beakers and opted to go back to my hotel instead.

Which is where I want to be—in my dry bed, with dry clothes and dry blankets and a dry book—not in the drenching rain with a barefoot little American. No matter how red her lips are. Or how enticingly her wet dress clings to her frame.

I scowl again.

"It's back that way," I say, pointing behind me. "Just around the corner."

"What?" she asks, clearly unable to hear me.

"It's back that— Oh, fuck it," I mutter, taking her by the elbow and yanking her into the deep doorway of a closed shop. The absence of the rain is almost as shocking as the presence of it, although it still rushes down next to us in a dull, silver roar.

"It's just past the corner there," I say again, and in the sheltered cove of the doorway, she can finally hear my words. "Left at the lights, then just a street down."

"Oh, good," she says, looking genuinely pleased. And also genuinely cold. Goosebumps pebble her bare arms and chest, and I make a valiant effort not to notice her nipples bunched tight under her dress.

A very valiant effort.

I fail, of course.

Her teeth chatter as she says, "Th-Thank you! My phone wouldn't work in the rain, and I thought I memorized the way, but it all looked different once I actually got here, and then the rain made it so hard to see—" Her own shivers break apart her words, and for some reason this makes me unaccountably annoyed.

"Here," I say gruffly, shrugging out of my jacket and putting it over her shoulders. She's flapping a hand in protest, but her hand stills as soon as the dry, warm interior of the jacket touches her shoulders. She practically folds herself into the jacket then, doing this thing where she rubs her cheek against the collar, and I know it's to get dry—*I know that*—but fuck if it doesn't look like she's nuzzling into it. Like a kitten against the warm palm of its owner.

"Thank you," says the girl, her eyes wide pools of deep blue. I notice with a strange curl of satisfaction that she's not shivering as hard now.

"Why don't you have a jacket?" I demand again, knowing I sound surly but refusing to care. Everyone else in my life has written me off as a miserable bastard and they ignore me as such—this girl might as well learn too.

At that, her mouth forms into a defensive little moue. "It's *June*," she says. "I shouldn't need a jacket in *June*."

I stare at her like she's insane, which maybe she is.

"And the bare feet?"

"My feet got wet," she says, as if this is an entirely adequate explanation. "I didn't like it."

"You realize they've gotten even wetter without shoes."

"It's better this way," she insists, waving her shoes at me. Once I see them, I have to agree. I don't see how anyone could walk in those across the width of the shoe shop, much less along slippery, uneven pavement.

"I hope whoever you're meeting sends you home in a taxi," I mutter.

"Oh, I'm not meeting anyone," she says.

"What?"

She reaches up to brush a wet strand of hair off her cheek, but I beat her to it. I don't know why, but it's instinctive, like breathing, like blinking. Touching her.

My fingertips linger on her cheek after I brush the hair aside, and she stares up at me with something too close to trust. I drop my hand.

"I only have one night in London," she says, all that trust and big-eyed nuzzling replaced by something matter-of-fact and utterly practical. "And I spent days researching where to go for a drink tonight. It had to be within walking distance of my hotel, it had to have several five-star reviews on multiple restaurant rating sites, and it had to be established enough to have regulars but new enough to be trendy. The Goose and Gander met all of those requirements."

Well, that's where research will get you. An obnoxious hipster cave of Edison bulbs and reclaimed wood.

"And why that specific criteria?" I ask, but I'm already peering back out into the rain, wondering if it's let up enough that I can send this crazy, shivering girl on her way. Get back to my night. My night in a dry bed with my book, alone.

Somehow it doesn't sound as appetizing as it did just a few minutes ago.

"Oh," she chirps, like she's pleased I asked. "I wanted to find a man to sleep with."

It takes a moment for her words to unfold in my brain, and I'm still staring at the rain when her meaning becomes clear. An unpleasant bolt of *something* hits me with a muffled thud.

My head swivels slowly back so I can look at her. "Excuse me?"

Her face is animated now, all red lips and high brows and dark lashes in the shadowed, rainy night. "Well, I have a plan, and I think it's a very good plan, but unfortunately my circumstances are narrowed to this one night in particular—"

"A *plan*."

She nods, that pleased look again, like I'm her star pupil.

Fuck that. *I'm* the professor here, and I have the sudden urge to tell her so. To press her against the wall and put my lips to her ear and murmur all the ways she'll respect my authority and experience.

My cock responds to the image, straining full and heavy at the thought of touching her. Teaching her. Punishing her.

"You see," she says, totally oblivious to the deviant lust pounding through me, "I really need a man with a willing penis—or I suppose I should say a willing man with a penis, but

16

when I say it like that, it sounds very dismissive of non— You're scowling again."

She's right. "So what you're saying is that you have a plan to go to a place you've never been, in a city you've never visited, to find a man you've never met to fuck you?" My voice is frigid, bordering on cruel, and I see her blanch.

"That's very judgmental," she scolds, but I'm not to be scolded. Not right now, because I do the scolding, I make the rules, and the sooner she learns that—

Wait, no, what am I thinking? She's not going to learn anything from me. I'm not going to teach her anything. I'm not even going to spend another ten minutes with this deranged, bedraggled girl.

Even if she has the kind of long, thick hair that begs to be wrapped around a fist. Even if she has a rain-chilled body just crying to be loved warm again.

Even if she has the kind of plush red lips designed to drive men mad.

But I've been down this road before, and I know what lies at the other end of it. Bitter memories and a life left in pieces.

Never again.

"I'm judgmental because it's an idiotic idea," I reply in a sharp voice. "Do you have any idea how unsafe that is? How foolish?"

Even in the dark, I see how heat glints in her eyes, and she sticks a finger in my chest as if she's about to deliver me a scathing lecture. As she does, her arm leaves the warm confines of my jacket and reveals a delicate wrist circled with a thin band of leather.

A watch.

I don't know why that's the thing that does it, but something shears off inside my mind, sending my control bumping and careening off the tracks.

"Where's your hotel?" I ask before she can start in on whatever she was about to say.

Her brows pull together and her mouth closes. Opens again. "Why?" she asks suspiciously.

"Because I'm taking you back there."

"Why?" she asks, genuinely confused now.

"Because there's no way in hell I'm letting you prance off to a bar to find some stranger to fuck you," I say. And I give her a brief once-over, my eyes tracing where the fabric of her dress clings to her breasts and her soft belly and her achingly shaped hips. There are no secrets through that wet fabric, and those shockingly abundant curves are on clear display for anyone with eyes. For the undoubtedly many willing penises back at the pub.

The thought makes my chest tighten with something uncivilized and jealous.

"Especially not looking like *that*," I add.

Her cheeks flush dark enough that it's visible even in the night shadows, and I realize too late she thinks I'm mocking her, not warning her.

Fine. So be it. If that's what it takes to save her from the greedy arseholes at the Goose and Gander, then I'll pay the price. "What hotel?" I repeat.

She worries her bottom lip between her teeth, and that simple act has my erection throbbing against the damp fabric of my trousers, begging to be let free, begging out to play. And oh, how it could play along the soft lines of her mouth and over the wet pink of her tongue. How rude and rough it would look against the overflowing handfuls of her tits...

"The Douglass," she says finally.

"I'm staying at the Douglass too," I say before I can stop myself, and then horror curls through my chest.

She's too close.

Too real.

Too...*possible.*

Would it be so bad? a tiny voice whispers in my mind. *Just one night with a girl you'll never see again?*

Yes, goddammit. Yes, it would.

Meanwhile, the girl seems to be having some sort of insight. Some sort of wild epiphany. "You," she says slowly.

"What?"

"You!" Her entire face lights up. "You could be the one!"

I stare at her. "You're joking."

She's too excited to catch on to the rhetorical nature of my statement, already bouncing on the balls of her feet. She's so short that even on her tiptoes, the top of her head barely clears my chin. "I'm not joking! It's perfect, don't you see? We're even staying at the same hotel! You can have sex with me and then just go right back to your room!" She beams up at me, as if expecting some kind of approbation for working out this problem of hers.

"You cannot be serious," I say in something very close to a stammer, which pisses me off. I'm *not* uncertain, I know how I feel about everything always, and I know how I feel about this:

the girl is mad and I'm leaving.

"I *am* serious," she says, brow furrowed, as if puzzled as to why that would even occur to me. "I would just like to have sex with someone tonight, and you're handsome and you're here."

And that's when I realize she's not mad. She's something much, much worse—she's innocent. And willing.

I turn to go, and she catches my arm, her little watch flashing in the shimmering glow of the streetlights. A stupid little watch that I bet she puts on every morning so she won't be late for whatever burlesque antics she has devised for that day. I bet she's on time for everything. I bet she's early to every class or meeting or shift, sitting with a straight back and with a pencil caught between her teeth, a spare pencil speared through a bun of soft, glossy hair...

Fuck.

I pull free of her arm. "Keep the jacket," I mutter, ducking back into the rain and away from this creature who seems to be built out of my most shameful temptations, every inch of me protesting at the distance between us, at pulling away from her.

But there's no other way. For the sake of her soul and mine, I should stay far away from her and her little watch and her wanton body with its big, soft curves and needy nipples.

The chilly rain sluicing down is a relief, soaking me straight through without my jacket and quelling the heat inside my blood just enough so I can think again. So I can remember the life I built, free of temptation, free of chaos, free of sin.

I take a deep, rainy breath. It's going to be okay. I was tested and came up with full marks. And now to my reward, which is a chaos-free night. Alone.

Fuck, what cold comfort. Comfort even colder than the rain soaking me through.

But the cost of giving in to my urges would make my life even colder still.

"You're not married, are you?" a voice comes from beside me.

I look over at the girl following me. She peers closely at me through the rain. "Girlfriend? Boyfriend?"

"I'm not married, and I'm not seeing anyone. *Not that it matters.*"

I try to walk faster, shoving my hands in my pockets and ducking my head from the rain, but she keeps up, nearly jogging now. My jacket hangs open enough that I can see what effect jogging has on the glistening rounds of her breasts peeking up over her bodice.

Christ.

"I'm not either," she says. "Married or dating, that is."

"It doesn't matter."

"Do you think I'm pretty enough to have sex with?" she says, her voice growing louder as a bus sloshes by.

"What?"

"I mean, if you're not attracted to me, I totally understand." She hops over a puddle in an expedient, unself-conscious move that almost makes me smile.

"Most men aren't attracted to me. That's why I had to come all the way to London to..." She trails off, clutching the jacket tighter around her. "Anyway," she continues in a defeated voice. "I'd understand if you weren't."

The lonely note in her voice draws me up short, even

though the safety of our hotel shimmers mirage-sweet just across the road.

I turn to her in the rain. "You think I'm not attracted to you?"

"Well, most guys—"

"I'm not most *guys*," I growl, and her lower lip goes between her teeth again. But not in fear like it should.

In interest. In desire.

She's too innocent by far.

"You think men don't want you?" I ask in a low voice, taking a step forward. She watches me with an eager trepidation, and it makes me harder than I thought possible. "Everything about your body reminds a man of fucking. Your tits, your mouth, those ridiculous hips. Even those big blue eyes of yours make a man wonder what they'd look like peering up at him with you on your knees. Looking at him from over your shoulder as he bends you over his desk." I stop abruptly, my words getting too personal, too tailored to my own fucked-up needs.

She releases that lower lip, and I'm nearly undone by how open she looks, how vulnerable. I want to sweep her into my arms and cover all that vulnerability with my body—protect her from the world even as I refuse to protect her from myself.

Get a fucking grip, Oliver.

This can't happen.

But what if it could? I won't ever have to see this girl again. She's not my student.

She's not Rosie, the little voice reminds me. *She can't hurt you.*

"Well, then it's simple," the girl says, as if she can read

my thoughts. "If you're attracted to my body and you're unattached—"

"It's complicated," I say, pushing past her to splash my way to the hotel. She has no idea how complicated.

She has no idea how *wrong*.

Like before, she follows me. "Please. I promise I'm not crazy. I'm just tired of—" She stops, seems to change her words. "Tired of not having sex. Please."

"It's for your own good," I mutter, even though my entire body is swirling with the need to give her what's *actually* for her own good, which is her over my lap, legs kicking adorably, as I redden her ass with my palm.

I'm so hard now. Hard enough that it must be obvious. Hard enough to be past caring. Hard enough that the minute I slip inside my hotel room, I'm going to have a hand braced on the door while my other fists my cock.

"How do you know what's for my own good?" the girl asks, and it's the way she asks that makes my steps falter. She doesn't demand it like most women would, and she doesn't deny that I *might*. That I might know what's for her own good and that I might know it well enough to tell her.

No.

No.

"We're not doing this," I tell her as we reach the doors of the Douglass, and I recognize how ridiculous it is that I'm holding the door open for this woman even as I'm trying to push her away. "You're just going to have to trust me."

She steps inside, and it's so bright that my eyes take a moment to adjust. When they do, I see that she's shoving my jacket at me.

"Here. Thank you for this, and take it back. And for the record, I *don't* trust you, and why should I? I'm a grown woman and I don't know you—and also I've done a lot of research about sex, so I'm pretty sure I know what I'm talking about."

She's gesturing now, the hand still clutching her shoes waving them around, but I'm not watching the shoes, I'm watching *her*—the almost embarrassingly generous curves of her. Not embarrassing because of the generosity but because of the near-wantonness of them. The illicit thoughts those curves conjure even fully clothed as she is.

Of course, *fully clothed* is a misleading term at the moment, because yes, that little waist and those lavish tits and hips are covered with fabric, but the wet dress clings to every contour and swerve of her body. I can even make out the gentle dip of her navel, the place where her thighs meet her body. The sweet bullets of her nipples.

Even the rest of her body is wanton: the long arch of her neck, still slicked with rain, the exposed square of her shoulders, the long wet hair that waves in dark webs down her back and over the elegant line of her collarbone.

Even her innocent anger feels tempting. Even the cocoon of inexperience around her drives me crazy.

Even that goddamn watch is irresistible.

I take my jacket and start walking to the lift. I have to put some space between us or my skin's going to catch on fire.

"Please?" she asks one last time. "*Please?*"

"No." I'm almost to the lift doors now, I'm almost safe.

Or rather, *she's* almost safe.

"Then I'm going to the Goose and Gander," she says,

frustrated. "Or *anywhere*. But I'm not giving up, not when I only have one night here."

I've already hit the button for the lift by the time she's uttered the words, but it's not too late to spin around and glare at her. "What did you just say?" I ask in a low voice.

She's already turning around, and I realize with some mixture of fury, horror, and lust that she *means it*. She's going to go back out into that gale. To find another man.

My hand finds her elbow, and I pull her into me with a growl. "You're not going anywhere."

She gives me a glare as turbulently aroused as my own, pressing her wet curves against me in something between a challenge and a request.

"What exactly are you going to do about it?" she dares.

My cock is a hot bar of steel between us, fussing at the seam of my trousers, and I can't help but press it into her belly. And my mouth is dry, so fucking dry, with wanting her. "Girls who disobey get punished," I warn.

"By you?"

"By me."

Suddenly, I find that I'm not holding her to me so much as she's holding herself to me, her high heels dropping to the floor in a dull clatter as her fingers find the flats of my chest under my thin sweater.

"Punishing bad girls... Is this you being kinky or a serial killer?" she asks, that red mouth curved in what could only be called impertinence.

I can barely breathe. And I can't even fathom saying the word *kinky* like she's just said it, like she would say *tall* or

English. Like it's nothing. Like it's no big deal.

Like she might want it.

All I choke out is a husky, "I'm not a killer."

She has no reason to believe me, no reason to believe that I'm safe, which is exactly why I didn't want her trawling for strange men in the middle of London.

And all thoughts sizzle and melt away in a searing instant because she's hooked her arms behind my neck and pulled herself up to my mouth.

Because she's kissing me with red, rain-spattered lips.

And I am done for.

CHAPTER THREE

ZANDY

He tastes like mint.

Not toothpaste mint, but fresh mint, straight from the garden, herbal and with the tiniest bit of cold sting. I moan the minute I taste it, the minute our tongues slide together, and his answering moan has me throwing all lingering doubts onto the floor along with my dumb shoes.

I don't care that I don't know him. I don't care that he's not the plan. I want it to be him. Him with his testy refusals. Him with his dark threats. Him with those hypnotic eyes that are every color and that mouth shaped somewhere between elegance and cruelty.

His hands are spread big and possessive on my back now, keeping me so tight against him that I can feel every flat, hard plane of his chest and stomach. I can feel the heavy ridge in his pants that tells me how much he meant his words from earlier in the rain.

Everything about your body reminds a man of fucking.

It's the first time I've ever thought of my body that way—of sexy instead of heavy, of desirable instead of softly messy. And I like it. I like how his eyes burned over my curves, as if he were already planning things that would take him straight to hell.

I want it to be him.

And almost like he reads my mind, he turns us and starts walking me backward into the elevator, pausing only to duck down and grab my shoes. Once we go through the elevator doors, he reaches for my thighs and lifts me up as if I weigh nothing, still kissing me with those soft, minty lips all the while.

Well, not kiss, really. *Devour* is more like it, as if he hasn't kissed a woman in years—as if he hasn't even *touched* anyone in years. He seems that hungry for it. But new to sex as I am, I know you don't kiss like him without vast experience, so surely he's not that hard up for it? Surely someone like him, handsome and mysterious and captivating, has someone in his bed every night?

Funny how the observation makes me jealous, given that I don't even know him. I don't even know his name. But even as I'm jealous of all the experience belied by his capable handling of me, I'm also grateful for it.

Grateful for the easy, knowledgeable way his hands work my body, pinning me between his leanly muscled frame and the wall of the elevator.

Grateful for the expert way he matches our bodies together, sliding me so that my lace-covered pussy grinds over the thick part of him that throbs for me.

Grateful for the smooth way he deepens our kiss, exploring my mouth, biting at my lips and my jaw, and leaving me a wriggling, wet mess.

"Which floor?" he growls into my mouth.

"Wh-What?"

"We're doing this in your room," he says, and it was always my plan to bring someone to my room for safety reasons, so I tell him.

"Nine."

He slams a fist against the wall of buttons, and then he's back to plundering my mouth, not so much coaxing me open as taking what he wants, and God, it's like nothing I ever could have dreamed. I've known lust myself. I've known what it feels like to have my body aching with the need for friction and fullness, but I've never, ever imagined *this*. The rush of power and pure biological frenzy of feeling someone *else's* lust. The way it threads through my own desire like a hot copper wire. The way it makes me want more, more, more.

And more.

I have almost no control over myself in this moment, grinding my needy core against him, rubbing my breasts against his chest, yanking everywhere at his sweater and his firm arms and shoulders and at the wet lengths of his hair—too short to be long but too long to be anything other than unkempt.

He lets me pluck and paw at him, and it seems to drive him madder and madder—his kisses growing more savage, his grip more merciless, until the elevator doors open and he drops me to my feet, yanking me into the hallway before I can find my balance.

"Nine thirteen," I manage, fumbling with my purse for my phone as I'm pulled down the hallway and then surfacing with it right before I'm crushed against my door and kissed within an inch of my life.

"Take a picture of me," he says breathlessly against my lips.

"I— What?"

He pulls back just enough so I can see he's serious. Those blue-green-brown eyes swirl with something stormy and pained. "Take a picture of me and send it to someone you trust." And then he rattles off a string of numbers. His birthday.

"Why?" I ask again, even though I suspect why.

"Surely," he says, raising one warm hand to grip my jaw and hold me close for another hard kiss, "with all your research, you know why."

"So someone knows I'm with you."

"So you'll be safe," he corrects gently, nipping at my neck and then meeting my gaze. "I don't know if I can ever forgive you for being so careless with yourself."

I laugh—half from his bossy words and half from the new flicker of his tongue along the shell of my ear. "My body is my own to be careless with."

"Not tonight, it isn't," he whispers. "Tonight it's mine."

I text his picture to a friend of mine, along with his birthday and name—*Oliver Markham*—and then I use the hotel app on my phone to unlock the door.

"What's your name?" he asks as we kiss our way into the room. I left a light on when I went out earlier, so I reach to turn it off because sex happens in the dark, I know that much, but he catches my wrist before I can do it. "Lights stay on," he rasps. "And I want your name. I told you mine."

That he did, and hell if Oliver Markham doesn't sound so fancy and English-y that I can hardly stand it. Suddenly I'm embarrassed of my own name, which seems to make me all the younger than the ten years I now know separate us.

"Amanda," I say, telling him my real name. No one calls me that—I've been Zandy since basically the moment I was born—but I file taxes as Amanda, and it does sound a lot more grown-up. Like the kind of name an Oliver would be paired with.

Oliver and Amanda sounds perfect.

Oliver and Zandy sounds like a joke.

"Amanda," he murmurs as his hands cup my face, his thumbs tracing soft lines along the rises of my cheekbones. "What do you want tonight?"

"I want you to have sex with me."

And that's all he needs.

His hands drop to my skirt, and they ruck up the wet fabric easily, hitching it all to my waist, and then he cups my pussy with one elegant hand. "You need to be fucked here? Hmm?"

"Yes," I sigh, trying to press into his hand. It feels so good, so fucking good, and I've never gotten this far...never had only a scrap of lace between my aching emptiness and a man's possessive touch.

But then his touch leaves my pussy, and I whimper. He reaches for the zipper of my dress and, with a practiced move, tugs it down. Before I can fully process what's happening, I'm bared to the waist, with only the thin silk of my bra between my body's secrets and his hungry eyes.

"But these need me too, don't they?" he says, his hands smoothing over the rounds of my breasts, shaping to their weight and ample size. Despite the cold and sharp cast of his mouth and the equally cold and aristocratic cut of his features, there's something almost boyish in his gaze as he cups and fondles me. Something awed and greedy. He slides the straps of my bra over my shoulders and then peels the damp silk cups from my skin.

"Christ," he mutters to himself as my nipples peek free and my breasts spill over the rest of the cups. "Jesus Christ."

And before I can say anything or even cover myself, like my instincts demand, his mouth is closing warm and wet over the needy tip of one breast, and I let out a noise that's nearly embarrassing in its shocked honesty. It's not the rehearsed coo of a woman in a porn video—it's a noise that comes straight from my belly, a low moan of unfiltered need.

I had no idea it could feel so good.

No idea.

His mouth is slick and warm, sucking every secret dirty wish of mine right to the surface of my skin as he works me and worries my nipple with rough nips and pulls.

I feel the wet response between my legs like nothing I've ever felt before. I mean, wet after a few minutes with battery power, sure, but wet from a stranger's mouth moving hungrily over my breasts? Wet from the flashing multicolored gaze of a man I don't know as he tears my dress down my hips and then scowls at my exposed form?

"You're so much," he says accusingly. "You're so fucking much."

I've always known that. I've always been so much. I'm the girl who raises her hand at the end of class because she can't bear for it to end. The girl who does every extra-credit assignment and then asks for more because she wants the teacher to like her. I'm curvy and eager and relentlessly energetic, and I've been those things ever since I can remember.

And yet never has being *too much* sounded like he's making it sound right now.

As if I'm a treasure and a curse all at once. As if he both loves and hates me.

As if I'm killing him simply by being myself and he wouldn't have it any other way.

Oliver circles me now, like a predator, like a wolf, and when I move to shift and put my arms over myself in a surge of self-consciousness, his hands are on me again, folding my wrists at the small of my back and locking them there with strong fingers.

"Bad girl," he murmurs into my ear, standing behind me so that all I have of him is that deliciously refined English voice and the warm grip of his hand. "Very bad girl."

"I'm not a bad girl," I protest, because his words are hooking somewhere deep inside me, somewhere deep inside the eager teacher's pet that is Zandy Lynch. Too late I remember I'm supposed to be Amanda, someone older and more sophisticated, someone who's been around the block and isn't as eager to please.

But it doesn't seem to matter. My eagerness to be a good girl for him seems to gratify, because he bites at my shoulder with a pleased noise.

"You want to be a good girl for me?" he asks. "You want to make me happy?"

"I do," I breathe. "I do, I do."

An approving growl at my ear.

I'm bent over the bed without so much as a warning; the only concession to my comfort is the pause he gives me to turn my head so I can breathe easily. And then my panties are ripped to my ankles and done away with.

"Red means stop," he says and kicks my legs apart.

I hold my breath, waiting for it...for something...for fingers or spanking or for him just to shove his cock right inside me. And oh shit, if he's going to do that, he needs a condom. But just as I'm about to tell him that, something utterly unexpected and utterly magical happens.

He runs his tongue soft and slick through the split between my legs, and I nearly jump up from the bed. A stinging slap to my ass makes me freeze.

"Good girls hold *still*," Oliver warns from behind me. I can feel the warm breath of his words against my pussy, a lurid reminder that he's able to see and smell and taste a part of me that no one has ever seen or smelled or tasted before, and I can't handle it. I can't even pretend to handle it. I squirm against the bed.

"Oliver," I moan, and it happens again. His tongue. His tongue and his lips and the intimate press of his nose into me, and I could peel apart with embarrassment, but he puts a hand on the small of my back and keeps me bent over the bed as he samples me.

I'm trapped. Trapped between his hands, which hold me down or spread me open depending on his whim. Trapped between the bed and his hungry mouth. Trapped between my embarrassment and just how insanely delicious it feels.

SIERRA SIMONE

Delicious because he thinks I'm delicious. Delicious because it's intimate and wet and hot.

Delicious because it's nothing like the familiar massage of my hands or the plastic hum of a vibrator. It's human and messy and dirty. It's not the tame thing I thought it was at all.

It's wild. It's primal. Like a lioness being pinned and bitten by her male. Like a cavewoman being slung over the shoulder of a lusty caveman. I thought I knew the boundaries of it. I thought my research would make the act planned and civilized...

There's nothing civilized about this. And despite his expensive sweater and even more expensive accent, there's nothing civilized about Oliver at all.

"I love the way you taste," he tells me, pulling back to bite at my ass. "Like summer. Fresh and tart and rich."

"I—" I have no words for this. Never in a thousand years when I made my plans and fantasized about finally having sex did I imagine what this would feel like—not just his mouth on my clit, but hearing him talk about my body with such raw pleasure, knowing that my secrets were secret no longer.

And never could I have imagined that he'd sit on the bed and then haul me over his lap like a child, his hand smoothing over the curve of my ass.

I look back at him, and he looks back at me with those uncannily colored eyes.

"Red means stop," he repeats.

And then he brings his palm down against my ass, and I buck over his lap.

"That is for going out alone in a strange city," he says as he tucks me even harder against his lap.

And spanks me again. "That is for looking for a strange man to fuck you."

And again. "And that is for being so fucking delicious that I couldn't say no when you asked."

I'm breathing hard into the blanket, the skin along my ass and thighs nearly dancing with sparks. There's heat everywhere—heat on my skin, heat deep in my muscles, heat in my belly, and heat between my legs.

I...I had no idea.

This definitely was not the plan. The plan never involved *spanking*. It never involved pain or punishment, and yet...when he soothes the skin with his hand, rubbing gently...when he croons that I'm a *good girl*, I'm more alive than I've ever felt. I'm dizzy with it and drunk with it, and I feel giddy and heady and wild. Like I can do anything and have anything.

Have anyone.

"I liked that," I murmur in disbelief. "I *liked* that."

His hand stops over my ass. "You did?" he asks in nearly as much disbelief.

I realize he's trembling where he touches me. His hands are shaking, and I can feel minute shudders chasing up and down his solid body.

I suddenly panic that I've done something wrong, that I've accidentally been disgusting by admitting that I liked it, but then he bends over me, pressing his lips to my back.

"Amanda," he groans and then bites me. "Where the hell did you come from?"

I don't know, but I'm suddenly encouraged. He's shaking

because of *me*. Because I liked what he did to me. I can't separate my enjoyment of it from his enjoyment of it, but maybe I'm not supposed to. Maybe that's the point.

And for once in my life, I'm happy not to overanalyze. Happy just to be in the moment and do something that feels good.

"More?" I ask, batting my eyelashes for good measure. "I know you've already spanked me for being a bad girl, but maybe some more just for fun?"

I don't have to ask twice.

A pleased noise rumbles deep in Oliver's chest, and he resumes his work—a bit lighter this time, I notice. Hard enough to sting but not so hard that it truly hurts. Soon I'm arching and squeaking with each strike, rocking back into his touch and also trying to press my pussy into the firm length of his thigh. His erection burns at my belly even through his pants, and he's breathing harder than I am—breathing like he's run a race, like he's pushed himself to the point of collapse.

And when the collapse comes, it's not his body but his control that fails. He scoops me up and tosses me back onto the bed, slouching over me like a lion in truth.

"Tell me you're wet," he says, lowering his body over mine and taking a nipple into his mouth. "Tell me you need it," he murmurs around my skin, leaving my nipple to kiss at the soft skin between my breasts and down the even softer contours of my belly. "Tell me you can't wait another minute." His mouth reaches my pussy, and it's like all the fire he's laid into my backside is now kindling here, here, *here*. And when he slides one long finger inside me, his lips and tongue and teeth all working to worship my clit, I'm done for.

Battery power has nothing on this.

My back bows off the bed as I cry out and grab for him, my fingers threading through his hair as I quiver and shake against his mouth, as my first ever non-solo orgasm tears through me with tidal, elemental power. I feel it everywhere—to the roots of my hair and in the balls of my feet—and as I'm racked with the gorgeous agony of it, he still pleasures me, still kisses and feasts on me like he can't bear to stop.

And when I finally, finally still against his lips, going from wire-tight to limp and happy, he gives my pussy a final kiss and rises up to his knees, tugging off his sweater and kicking off his shoes and trousers. He should look clumsy, pulling off damp clothes, but in that mysterious Oliver way, it all looks graceful. Powerful. And inch by inch, his body appears. His handsomely squared shoulders and deceptively wide chest and a torso ridged with lean muscle and marked with a single line of dark hair trailing down from his navel.

And then those hips, trim and narrow, the spread of dark hair low, low on his belly, the tops of firm thighs, and then—

Jesus, Mary, and Joseph.

His cock.

It flexes as I trace it with my gaze, the veined thickness, the blunt swell of the head, and the proud jut of its hardness. There's something so potent and arresting about this part of him; it's so very male and handsome, and even just looking at it makes my belly churn low with new longing.

"You want it," Oliver says, drawing my gaze up to his. It's not a question, but I answer anyway.

"Yes."

He looks down at my pussy, spread and wet, and then up to my face. I can't read his expression, but there's something twisting the sharp corners of his lips, and I realize it's excitement. I realize it's glazed fervor.

He wants me as much as I want him.

And God, how that punches me in the gut.

"I wear condoms," he informs me, reaching for his wallet.

"Okay."

"Every time."

"Okay."

He tears the wrapper open with long fingers, nimble and dexterous in the way that brings to mind writing or piano playing, and then rolls the latex sheath over himself with an ease that both fascinates and frustrates me.

"And I'm on top this time."

"Okay by me." And it really is because I'd have no idea what the hell to do if I were on top. And being so exposed— not just with my braless breasts and my soft thighs but with my inexperience, with my unpracticed movements... I don't think I'm ready for that yet. Especially not with someone as wickedly sophisticated as Oliver.

"Any other rules?" I tease, even though I like the rules. I've always liked rules, and from him, there's nothing sexier.

"Yes," he says, crawling back between my legs. "Red still means stop."

And then he lays his body over mine, matches the wide crest of himself to my cunt's opening, and begins to push inside.

I arch in a slow writhe, the pressure too much, the bite

of pain too real, and for a substantial moment, I think about pushing him away. I think about saying *red*. It's one thing to read about the discomfort some women face in their inaugural encounters with penetration, but it's an entirely different thing to feel it. It's so unfamiliar, this discomfort. It's so intimate, right at the heart of me, as if I'm being split open by the coolly vicious man above me.

Except not vicious.

Not really.

Even as he spanked me, he soothed me and played with my pussy, and even as he wedges inside me now, he strokes the hair from my face and sucks at my neck. And the noises he makes as he grits his teeth and pushes in—guttural noises, animal noises, words uttered in the most filthy tone possible: *tight, Jesus, tight* and *goddammit, you feel so good* and *so fucking much, so fucking much.*

"Going to fuck you," he whispers into my neck as his head drops to the pillow next to mine. He's still only halfway in. "Going to fuck you until you're a good girl again."

All of it, all of it, but especially those last words, take the pinch of pain and turn it into something new. Something as good as the good girl I want to be for him, and instead of pushing him away, my hands wander down to the tight clench of his ass and coax him in farther. Deeper. Until he's seated as deep as a man can go in a woman.

"Oliver," I gasp, because he's filling me where I've never been filled, heating me and stretching me and stroking me, and the tip of him is kissing against a part of me I never even knew was there. "Oh, Oliver. It feels— I can't believe how it feels."

He pulls up and stares down at me, that sharp-tipped mouth pressed into a line and his eyebrows furrowed. "I can't believe how *you* feel," he corrects. And then he shakes his head slightly, his mouth twisting in some conversation with himself. "You're not at all what I expected," he says. "You're not at all how you look."

"How do I look?" I whisper.

He gives a dark smile and reaches up to run a thumb over my fire-engine red lips and then down over a plump breast. "Like you know everything there is about fucking."

"I don't know anything," I admit. It was never the plan to reveal my virginity to my would-be paramour, and it seems strange to tell Oliver about it now, when he's already inside me. But a big part of me wants to tell him, wants him to know how much I'm trusting him with, how much I need him to continue being his mixture of safe and dangerous. But then I add, "You have to show me. Have to teach me," and his eyes go so dark, so feral, that I decide the conversation can wait until later.

I want him ferocious now. I want him looking like this, all possessed and desperate.

"You want me to teach you?" he rasps, moving between my legs again. "You want to be my little student? My little whore?"

Holy shit. I nearly come from his words alone—from this teacher game, this good-girl game. And still he moves, long and sweet strokes that have my toes curling and my back arching.

"Good girls come on the cocks their teachers give them," Oliver says as he fucks me. "You want to be a good girl, don't you?"

I nod vehemently. It's all I want, it's all I'll ever want, and I need to be his good girl. I need it like I need air and water and breath. "Please," I whimper. "Help me be a good girl, please, please."

He moves the wide pad of his thumb to my clit between us, rubbing in time to his deep, rolling thrusts, and the orgasm builds like nothing I've ever felt. A runaway train bearing down on me, a wall of sweaty, dirty pleasure—it's so much that I try to move away from it, try to squirm away from under him.

I can't bear it. I know I can't. I'll die if I orgasm, because it's too strong, too fucking strong, it will shake the bones right out of my body.

"Oh no, you don't," Oliver murmurs, his body easily chasing mine, his thumb on my swollen pearl all the while. "You give it to me first. You let me have it."

And I can't resist him—not the thick bar of needy male inside me, not his polished accent, not his still-damp hair tousled around his face. Not his savage mouth or his kaleidoscopic eyes. He stills me just enough for the climax to nip at my heels, to tackle me down, and with a panicked moan, I'm felled by it.

I'm slayed by it.

It starts in the deepest pit of my belly, right around the wide tip of him, crushing in and then exploding out like an atom bomb, crumpling through me like I'm nothing but paper in a strong fist. I can feel myself clenching—my belly and my thighs and the inner parts of me—squeezing and clutching at his erection, and he hisses, long and wounded, his hands fisting hard enough in the pillows around my head that I can hear the stress of the fabric. And I can't speak, I can't ask if his reaction is good or bad, but there's something in the rigid tension of his torso, in the strained cords of his neck, that make me think it's good, that he's getting pleasure from my pleasure just as I did from his when he spanked me.

"Dammit," he says through gritted teeth. "God*dammit.* I'm going to—you're making me—Amanda—"

The last comes out as a jagged groan, and then he's up on his knees, his hands curling hard over my hips as he fucks his way through his own climax. His eyes flutter closed, so I can watch him in my state of limp stupefaction as he uses my body to his own ends. As he uses my happy pussy to send himself over the edge. And then with a grunt and the impossible tightening of all those delicious muscles in his arms and chest and belly, he stills, buried to the hilt, as he pulses in fast, flexing throbs.

"Fuck," he mumbles, his head dropping down to hang between his shoulders. His eyes are still closed, and I shamelessly drink him in: the tightly carved body and the wide root of his cock just barely visible below the rise of my cunt. The furrowed pull of those dark eyebrows, as if his own pleasure is a problem he's trying to mentally work out, and the soft part of his lips, as if something about this has rendered him unexpectedly vulnerable. The nearly too-square jaw and the high cheekbones—giving his face a geometric cast normally only seen in marble busts—and the vaguely unkempt hair that waves over his neck and temples.

I'm curious about his hair, which is gorgeous but obviously neglected. I'm curious about his hands, strong but pale, as if they rarely see the sun. And I'm curious about his lean body and his earlier self-denial and his obvious kinky side.

I'm curious about *him*. I want more of *him*.

Oh.

Oh no.

I've read about this. I've researched this. This is the inevitable rush of connection that comes from all the oxytocin Oliver's stoked in my blood. He's flooded me with hormones, and now those hormones are insisting that I form a human bond with him, and that's why people get snuggly and all clingy after sex.

Well, that's not going to happen with me. That's not the plan. And given what I know about Oliver, I doubt it's his plan either.

I'm not going to be curious.

I'm not going to want him.

He solved my problem, and that's that.

I'm so busy reminding myself that all this affection and vulnerability is hormone-based and therefore not real that I don't notice he's opened his eyes and is staring back down at me.

"Amanda," he says huskily.

I don't know what to say back because the research didn't cover this.

Do I say his name back? Do I offer him my shower? Do I tell him I don't expect him to stay?

But before I can decide, he circles himself with a finger and thumb and makes to pull out of me, and I bite my lip at the sudden sting.

He freezes, and I realize that he's looking with some worry

44

at the pain on my face, and then with slow horror, his gaze goes to his cock.

Even from here, I can see the remnants of my innocence smeared on the condom.

"Oliver," I say quickly. "I can explain."

CHAPTER FOUR

OLIVER

I have to get her blood off me, and I have to—I don't even know what I have to do. Clean her. Clean myself. Offer to lash my own back. Whatever it is you do when you've accidentally fucked a virgin.

Shit.

Shit.

It makes so much sense now. Her little gasps of surprise let out at the smallest things. Her expression of wonder as I serviced her cunt. Her wide, vulnerable gaze as I slowly stretched her open. Stretched her open for the first time.

And I'm going to hell because guilt is not the first thing that races through me.

It's excitement.

It's more lust, stiffening my spent cock.

It's a dark possession, growling and flexing claws in my chest, telling me she's mine mine *mine*.

I ignore these though, holding up a hand to stay her words as I climb off the bed and rid myself of the condom. I've forgotten how wet sex is, how messy, although given how long it's been, I'm shocked I remember anything.

I walk back to the bed, tracing the lines of her body with my eyes because I can't help it. She's some kind of vision like this, her dark hair tangled everywhere in lovers' knots and her body a topography of pure adolescent fantasy—lush tits, a nipped-in waist, and hips in a decadently feminine spread.

And then there's the blood on the inside of her thighs. The questions in her deep blue eyes. The lingering redness around the sides of her hips reminding me of how she felt over my lap, squealing and writhing as she took her punishment.

I spanked a *virgin*. Oh God.

"I'm getting a cloth for you," I say. "Stay here." It comes out sterner than I mean it to—sterner than it should have, given what I've just robbed from her—but the immediate acquiescence in her gaze whisks the follow-up apology right off my lips. And replaces it with a noise of approval.

She is such a good student.

I quickly clean myself in the bathroom and then bring out a fresh warm cloth for her, thinking I'll hand it to her and let her clean herself, but as I approach, she parts her legs for me, as if it's the most natural thing in the world. As if it's my due.

My cock jolts again, bobbing at visions of a future that will never happen: of this girl spreading her legs for me whenever I ask, offering up her sweet body like it's mine to take. Sucking my cock under my desk while I work. Writing lines at her own desk, naked and ashamed. Crawling over my lap whenever I need it, letting me pet and tease and spank that round ass until she's begging for relief.

No, Oliver. It's a miracle she didn't run away screaming

the moment I bent her over the bed. There's no way a nice girl like her—a barely non-virgin, a girl with a watch—would ever want to play my sick games.

But I let myself have this moment where I clean her myself. Where I spread her even more, carefully, see to her tender skin. Roll her over and check her bottom, even though I took it fairly easy on her. The funny thing is that after all these years, "fairly easy" was still enough to nearly make me come in my pants. And it was her who made it that way. Her gratifying little moans and tempting little wriggles. The way she said *I liked that* with such pleased surprise. With such innocent abandon.

Fuck.

It's not a good thing the way it makes me feel. As if I'm not so lonely. As if I can have...this.

She sighs as I clean her, and after I put the washcloth over the towel bar in the bathroom to dry, I wonder what comes next. The last time I slept with a virgin, I was a fumbling virgin myself, and whatever followed the too-short act is blurred by enough awkwardness and time that I can barely remember it. I have no idea what to do as a man. As a polite and—dubiously—civilized man.

And so I debate whether I should apologize or get dressed or what, and then she holds out her arms.

"I know it's just the oxytocin," she says sleepily. "But I'd like you to hold me for a minute. You don't have to stay long, just—" She yawns, those red lips stretching hypnotically, her tongue so temptingly wet and pink. "Just for a few minutes until I can metabolize these hormones."

I should hesitate. I *would* hesitate with any other woman. I don't do holding, I don't do postcoital anything except shame and regret, and yet somehow I'm climbing into the bed with her. Somehow I'm sliding under the covers and folding her into my arms, and somehow I'm not balking at the familiar way she nestles into me, as if she belongs there.

Somehow I'm relaxing around her. Somehow I'm enjoying the way she feels like this, with her head pillowed on my chest, her curves smashed against me, and her cheek rubbing against me like a needy cat's.

I should leave.

I should say I'm sorry—for the spanking and for the barbaric way I fucked her—and then I should leave. And I'm going to.

In just a minute.

After I've enjoyed the sated warmth of her for a little longer. After I've gotten my fill of her scent, all deep floral and spice.

After I've rested my eyes and given in to the strange peace she's infected me with.

I really am going to leave.

I really am...

♦ ♦ ♦ ♦

The sunshine breaks through the room with a sheepish kind of warmth, as if embarrassed to wake me up, and it's pure instinct that makes me reach for the woman in bed with me. Well, pure instinct and a painfully erect cock, aching from a night of dreams about an American girl who likes spanking and spreading her legs for me.

But my fingers encounter nothing but cool sheets, and when I open my eyes, I see groggily that I'm alone.

Suddenly, I'm not so groggy. The entire shameful night floods back into my memories. What I did to Amanda, what I took from her. Falling asleep uninvited like an idiot.

What a cretin she must think I am...what a monster.

And she's not wrong. I am a monster.

I sit up, and it should relieve any person to see what I see next, which is a hotel room bereft of the effects of its occupant. No more suitcase on the stand. No laptop situated neatly on the desk. When I go to the bathroom, the space is as clean as it must have been when she rented it, a still-wet shower and sink the only evidence that she was here.

That and a note propped against the mirror.

Oliver, it reads in a neatly printed hand.

I'm sorry if last night caused you any worry, but I wanted you to know it was better than I ever could have dreamed. We won't see each other again, but I'll never forget how good you made me feel. I'm proud to have been your good and bad girl, even if only for one night.

—Amanda

My chest feels heavy with something unfamiliar, and I find myself rubbing idly at it as I set the note down. Pick it up and read it again.

Fold it and put it in my jacket pocket—so the hotel staff won't find it, I tell myself—but after I dress and leave the room, I find myself touching it. Rereading it as I ride the lift down to my own floor to change clothes and shower. Running my fingers along the edges as I walk to the British Museum to meet a friend helping me with some research at one of the libraries there.

I'll never forget how good you made me feel.
I'm proud to have been your good and bad girl.
Even if only for one night.

This should be a good morning. I blew off some steam with a girl who let me practice all manner of depravities upon her, and then when I woke up, she was gone. No dangling expectations; no awkward send-off. Just a sweet note that was meant to assuage me of my guilt and firmly close the door on the possibility of more.

Which—excellent, right? The last thing I need is some curvy, blunt American invading my thoughts while I have important work to do. Invading my space with her wanting to be spanked and her mumbling about oxytocin and her fucking *watch*.

Last thing I need.
All for the best.
Right.

CHAPTER FIVE

ZANDY

The oxytocin isn't wearing off. Or at least it's not wearing off the way I thought it would.

I'm frowning at the glass of my train window as the countryside swishes by—flattish fields studded with animals and telephone poles, just like in Kansas—and I'm feeling an inconvenient restlessness, like I've left something important back in London. Something back in bed with Oliver.

Stop it.

It's not like he's a phone charger or a passport. I don't need him for anything else while I'm in the country, and this...this... *mooning* over him is immature. And if there's any advantage to losing my virginity at the ripe old age of twenty-two, it should be that I know better.

But it's weird, this feeling. It's immune to logic; it defies knowing better. I find myself smiling whenever I shift in my seat and the secret aches inside me declare Oliver's touch. I find myself biting my lip as I replay the fire and frenzy of his hand on my ass. And I squirm when I remember his words.

Good girls hold still.

Good girls come on the cocks their teachers give them.

Jesus.

But I do manage to stop myself from searching for Oliver Markham on social media. There's no point. Even with all these infatuated thoughts pinging around my brain, I know I'd never be so crazy as to track him down and reach out. My research indicated those things are unwanted. Considered clingy.

So I put my phone away and watch as the fields outside London slowly fold into rich, slow worlds of green trees and far-off church spires, and there's nothing Kansas-like about the view anymore. And with no homework and my job for Professor Graeme not yet started, I find myself in the luxurious position of having nothing to do.

I doze off to the gorgeous green view and the slow shake of the train.

And when I do, I dream of Oliver.

The rain is making it hard to hear my dad's voice. I press the phone closer to my ear and squint through my clear umbrella at the house in front of me—a white, thatched affair with deep windows and riots of flowers crowding the front.

"I said, did you make it to Graeme's house okay?" Dad repeats. "I should have done a better job with the timing or had him pick you up in London."

He sounds nervous, which is always how my father sounds. He teaches Victorian social history at the University of Kansas, and he's more comfortable in his cluttered office or in front of a whiteboard than he is in the real world, and these kinds of situations, even secondhand, tend to stress him out.

"The timing is fine, Dad. I wanted to have a night in London, remember?"

He makes a fretting noise. "I just wish he were there now to help you get settled in."

Professor Graeme scheduled an impromptu research trip to London after I'd already booked my flight, and I assured Dad—and told him to tell the professor—that I honestly didn't mind being by myself for the weekend. I mean, a chance to rattle around an adorable old cottage and explore the gorgeous sights of the Peak District? I'd *pay* to do that, so the opportunity to do so for free is not a hardship.

"I'll be fine," I soothe. "I can find my way to the kitchen and the bathroom, and that's all I need."

"Well, okay," Dad says in a worried tone. "You call me if you need anything. Graeme is a good man, but he's always been a bit reserved and not a little distracted. I can't imagine he'll be a very attentive host."

"Dad, you didn't set this up so I could sample English hospitality. You set it up so I could have hands-on experience with a private collection before I start library school." I walk up the flagged path to the front door, looking for the bright-blue flowerpot that should be hiding the key. "And if I can handle you, I'm sure I can handle him."

Whether man or woman, fussy old scholars are all the same. And I should know, because after my mom died, my father's fellow professors basically became my second family. I've spent my entire life around the species, and I'm incredibly grateful my dad's extensive network of academic colleagues yielded the chance to spend my summer in one of the most beautiful corners of the world.

However, I *have* adjusted my expectations to include all the things that living with an old person working on a book will mean.

Terrible television shows.

Stale store-bought cookies.

Finicky and exacting demands on my time.

But it will be worth it.

I say goodbye to Dad and let myself inside the house, parking my suitcase and wet umbrella carefully by the door so I don't drip water all over the clean flagstone floor. And then I step through the narrow hallway into the house of my dreams.

The flagged hallway is lined by bookshelf after bookshelf, each one crowded with a combination of well-worn paperbacks and sleek leather volumes and colorful modern hardcovers. The librarian's itch I feel to sort them is pure joy, pure brain-lust. I could spend hours poring over these shelves...and I will, I decide right then. I'll ask Professor Graeme if I can shelve these in my spare time, while I'm not helping him catalogue research. It would take me several delicious days to decide on a method, weighing my options between the traditional Dewey or a contemporary, more intuitive scheme...

I force myself on, past the sitting room overlooking the front garden full of flowers, past the snug with its cozy fireplace, and into the kitchen. It's massive and rambling and beamed and flagged and vaguely cluttered in a way that speaks to home and hearth rather than true untidiness.

I follow the stairs up to find three bedrooms—two of which

are clearly guest rooms, with narrow beds and nondescript furnishings, and the last is obviously Professor Graeme's. I feel a little guilty peeking inside, but I tell myself it's simply for orientation's sake as I get to know the house. In any case, there's not much to see. A large bed with an IKEA-looking duvet. An end table stacked with books. Sheepskin slippers tucked by the bed.

Slippers.

Well, if that's not a marker of advanced age, I don't know what is.

It's only as I leave his room and walk back down the hall that I realize I haven't seen any pictures anywhere. There are *paintings*—small landscape-ish things that have that unmistakable "acquired by a grandmother" look—and a bust of Charles Dickens with untold years of dust caught in the bronze curls of his beard, but no pictures of Professor Graeme himself. No long-dead wife or kids or grandkids, no obligatory picture frames with nieces and nephews.

Nothing.

That's a little strange, right?

Mulling over this, I hop down the stairs and find my way to the back of the house, which is dominated by his study. Where I imagine most of the working and cataloging will be. Like the curious cat I am, I push the already cracked door open farther and step inside.

It's a mistake.

The opening door sends a pile of books and pamphlets scattering across the rug—not that there's much room to scatter, given that there are piles and piles of books and paper *everywhere.*

Old books. New books. Rare books. Pamphlets that should be in clear archival envelopes or at least under glass. Folders upon folders of what appear to be photocopies. And a cat. Who opens her eyes at my appearance, stretches all her paws out to the same point, and then rolls over so her belly's in the air.

And goes back to sleep.

There is a small desk off to the side—mine, I should think... or it will be mine—and a large desk that's no less cluttered than the floor but at least shows signs of rudimentary organization. An old-fashioned ink pen lies across a closed leather notebook, a blotting paper and inkwell nearby, which does nothing to revise my assessment of his age. And behind the desk, there's a wide line of windows, stretching nearly the width of the room, showing nothing but silver rain at the moment.

I sigh at the room, at the rare books left carelessly on the floor and the Victorian documents moldering among photocopies and a sleepy cat, and I feel a librarian itch that's not so pleasant. None of these things will last if they're not properly taken care of, and between organizing, cataloging, and—now, I can see—preservation efforts, I don't think I'm going to have any time at all for the books in the hallway.

Or anything else.

I leave the books and the cat and finally walk through a glassed-in conservatory to the back of the house, where a jewel-green lawn studded with wildflowers leads down to the shallow River Wye. Even in the rain, the colorful stones under the water seem to sparkle and flash, and I think of Oliver's eyes. Green and blue and brown.

And after I remember his eyes, it's impossible not to

remember his hand sowing fire along my backside, his lips on my mouth and my neck and my breasts.

His lips lower down.

The sounds he made as he came.

With an abrupt turn, I leave the river and trudge back to the house through the rain.

Soon there will be too much work to do to think of Oliver Markham and his every-color eyes.

♦ ♦ ♦ ♦

I spend the weekend busily, if not entirely happily. I walk the mile or so to Bakewell and enjoy my first Bakewell tart— or pudding, as I am briskly informed it's called here. I visit Haddon Hall and enjoy the massive blooming roses with the fat bees doddering around them, and then I have tea at Chatsworth with only myself and a book. I walk the rambling paths around the vales of the Peak District, challenging in the kind of way that makes you grateful to have a drink at the end of the day but easy enough to walk in a dress like the ones I usually wear.

The cat has been left with plenty of food, but I treat her to bits and pieces of chicken from the sandwiches I get in town, and she sleeps on my lap in the evening as I read in the snug.

I absolutely, positively don't think of Oliver.

Not whenever I catch a glimpse of the river that reminds me of his eyes. Not when I peel off my damp clothes and remember how it felt to be undressed by him. Not in bed, where my curious fingers explore my secret soreness and try to mimic the feel of a haughty man's mouth.

Not at all, not at all, not at all, until finally on Sunday night, I kick off my covers and climb out of bed. It's late—close to eleven—but I don't care. I'm sick of masturbating in an old man's guest room. Sick of remembering Oliver's cool, cultivated voice. Sick of pretending I'm too sophisticated to care that the man I coaxed into bed is also mysterious, English, and handsome beyond belief.

It's like Oliver was some kind of vampire, and now I'm bitten. Now I'm doomed to crave his touch for eternity.

Ugh. And now he's turning me into the kind of girl who makes stupid metaphors!

I'm stopping this shit right now. I'm going to put so many things inside my brain that there won't even be room for Oliver Markham and his perfect body.

Dad said Professor Graeme wouldn't get in until tomorrow morning at the earliest, so I don't bother to change out of my camisole and sleep shorts. Instead, I walk downstairs huffing to myself, doing a little dance across the cold flagstone floors until I get to the study and its many cozy rugs. That cat comes with me, oblivious to the cold floors, walks up to a pile of yellowing newsprint and kneads it pointlessly for a minute, and then lies down.

I walk around the room, hugging my arms around myself to ward off the clammy night chill. I poke at some of the stacks with my toes, trying to get a feel for what the professor's research seems to encompass. I know he probably won't want me to start on anything in earnest until he arrives, but I can at least start sorting some of it and making lists of things to do and archival materials to order. But I have to be doing *something*.

I have to keep my thoughts occupied. Otherwise Oliver will creep into them again, and I can't have that.

The thing is that I've never had any trouble achieving something I've set my mind to. Honor roll, valedictorian, grad school of my choice—everything has boiled down to research and focus and discipline. I'm excellent at those things. I'm an excellent student.

So it was easy to promise myself that I'd be the perfect virgin. I'd be honest but not too honest, enthusiastic but not needy. I'd be able to shelve away the experience like a book and be able to revisit it with fond, wise memories. There was no reason to think I wouldn't be excellent at this either. But I'm not.

The thought makes me shuffle papers and books around a little harder than I should, sending dust clouding up into the air and stacks slumping sideways, much to the irritation of the cat, who looks at me over her shoulder and flicks her tail in a very deliberately unimpressed way.

"Oh sure," I tell her. "It's so easy to judge a girl when all you have to do is nap and eat."

Another tail flick. I glare at her.

"You know, this wouldn't be such a mess if your owner would clean up after himself," I grumble. "Why would anyone keep an office in this state? Or their research?"

"Because I like it that way," a cold voice says from behind me.

And I spin around to see the furious face of Oliver Markham.

CHAPTER SIX

OLIVER

It was a hard trip home.

Literally.

I spent my time on the train with crossed legs and gritted teeth, and then it took some artful draping of my jacket over my arm to cover my, ah, situation as I climbed onto the late bus from Matlock. And it isn't until right now, at my front door—tired and frustrated, a heavy bag full of photocopies and clothes slung over my shoulder—that I remember.

That I fucking remember.

The girl. Michael Lynch's girl.

Shit.

Lynch is an old acquaintance of mine. First my professor, when I spent a year studying abroad in America during my undergraduate degree, and then later a colleague and peer as we corresponded back and forth about various topics within our closely related fields. In one exchange, I made passing mention of needing an assistant simply to wade through all the material and make sense of it. It was a throwaway comment, bordering on a joke. Until Lynch wrote me back, offering up his librarian daughter for the cost of room and board.

He talked about the girl frequently—the fond asides of a proud father but not much more. To be honest, I forgot she existed until he mentioned her.

Zandy.

I pictured a girl looking like Michael—beanpole thin and bespectacled—poking around my research and asking all sorts of nosy questions about my methods, and I almost immediately said no. I enjoyed Michael's correspondence and his company, but I took this damn sabbatical from teaching precisely so I *wouldn't* have to talk to strangers. And that included any timid, mousy Lynch offspring inside my home. Inside my sanctuary.

But I owe Michael. He's been a good friend all these years, even after Rosie happened, even after I took a break from teaching—and, well, I really *do* need the help, if I am being honest. What started as a small stack of research beside my laptop has now become a behemoth of paper and ink that is happily swallowing up the rest of my study. Walking inside it is starting to put me in a bad mood—fine, a *worse* mood—and even my cat, Beatrix, seems to be losing patience with the unstable stacks of books, which have the tendency to slide and collapse under her feet when she tries to climb them.

Michael deserves the favor, and I deserve the help.

So I said *yes* and steeled myself to the thought of the summer with a girl bound to be as awkward and fretful as her father. It's only two months, and surely Michael would prepare his daughter for what a cold, miserable bastard I am. Surely she wouldn't take it personally.

I'd made my peace with Zandy's presence before I left for London, but now...

Now there's been Amanda.

And there's no peace left inside me. None at all.

In the moonless summer night, the lights inside the cottage burn a merry, welcoming yellow, although I can't help but rather grimly think of what I'll find inside. I repeatedly charge myself to be *nice*—or polite at the very least—and I remind myself that none of this is her fault. Not that I met a woman. Not that the woman let me play wicked games with her. Not that the woman let me deflower her and then somehow lulled me to sleep with soft curves and a faintly spicy smell.

It's certainly not her fault that I can't get this woman out of my head and that I'm strangely upset she left me that morning. Strangely bothered by the finality in her note.

We won't see each other again.

Why does that sting so much?

At least my lingering hard-on has settled down. It's a small comfort as I unlock the front door, unshoulder my bag, and step inside. I expect Beatrix to come whining for food as she usually does, but the front hall remains empty as I shut the door and shuck off my jacket.

She must be with the girl.

It's late, near midnight, and the girl should be in bed. Given all the lights, however, I assume she's in the snug or the kitchen, reading perhaps. Michael's always said he's a night owl himself, so perhaps it's fair to assume Zandy is the same.

When I get to the snug, though, she's not there. Nor is she in the kitchen. Maybe she went to bed and left the lights on for me?

But then I see it from the back hall off the kitchen—the

light coming from under the study door. Suddenly all of the dread about this arrangement comes roaring back. All of the frustration about Amanda. And I hate that someone's in my study while I'm not in there, touching my things without my permission.

I stalk to the study door, ready to kick it down and roar like a true Bluebeard, when I hear a low voice talking. A woman's alto, with a hint of rasp around the edges. I wonder if she's talking on the phone, but then I hear her pause to wait for a response, and Beatrix meows.

The girl is talking to the damn cat.

It shouldn't be so irritating, really, this familiarity with my cat, but it is. She's already in my study. She's already touching things she shouldn't be. And for my only companion to be drawn into this flagrant violation of hospitality? It's infuriating.

I'm going to eviscerate her for this. I'm going to make her regret ever setting foot in my private space and making friends with my cat. I don't care how ridiculous that sounds. It's still forbidden!

I start to open the door. And freeze.

I'm not greeted with the sight of some scrawny, owlish bookworm. No, I'm greeted with a heart-shaped bottom that begs to be pulled over my lap. And a narrow waist and lush breasts and—bloody Nora—no bra. She's only in a thin camisole and some very short sleeping shorts, moving on all fours at an angle away from me, her long dark hair spilling in luscious waves and breaking over her shoulders.

No, not scrawny at all. She's a siren. She's...she's...

She turns as she chatters to the cat and I see her face for

the first time. No lipstick, but I'd remember those plush, sinful lips anywhere.

The girl inside is not Michael Lynch's daughter.

She can't be.

Because she's Amanda.

My Amanda.

◆ ◆ ◆ ◆

"Why would anyone keep an office in this state? Or their research?"

My voice is harsh. "Because I like it that way."

She spins with a gasp, dropping the book she was holding. I don't trust myself to take another step inside, not sure if I'd take her over my knee or fuck her senseless. But I do know one thing. I thought I was furious before?

It's nothing compared to now.

"What the fuck are you doing here?" I demand. "Are you stalking me?"

Her face goes from confused to stung in an instant. Then to angry. "I think the real question is what are *you* doing here?" she asks. And then she reaches for one of the pokers still hanging by the disused fireplace. She waves it at me. "I'll—I'll call the police. And the professor. He's supposed to be back any minute now. He just went out to the...the store...and if he comes back and finds an intruder, he'll get the police for sure!" Her voice is warbling higher in her hysteria, and I'm so bemused by the poker situation and the way she's talking about me like I'm in the third person and all the *lies* she's telling and has told, that it takes me a moment to realize she doesn't know

I'm Professor Graeme.

She thinks I'm the intruder. She thinks I might hurt her.

Which—no. Never. I would never raise a hand against her.

Except if you've got her over your knee, a silky voice reminds me. Visions of her rump under my palm fill my head, and I know the voice is right.

"I fucking live here," I say. "This is my fucking house. Now do you want to explain what the bloody hell you're doing inside of it? After that little note? 'We'll never see each other again'? Did you steal my credit card information too?"

"You do *not* fucking live here. Professor Graeme does, and Professor Graeme is an old man. He's friends with my father and has slippers and everything!"

Well, now I think she's gone truly insane.

Except...

"Friends with your father," I repeat. I stare at her. "Your father is Michael Lynch?"

The tip of the fire poker lowers the slightest amount. "Yes," she answers, her eyes narrowing. It has the unfortunate—for me—effect of making her eyelashes sweep lower, long and sooty against her cheeks.

"Are you Zandy Lynch?"

The poker lowers a bit more. "Yes," she says.

"You told me your name was Amanda."

She drops the poker all the way down but still holds on to it, as if she's ready to strike me at any moment. "It is Amanda. Zandy's my nickname."

"It's still a lie."

"It's not," she fires back. "And you said your name was

Oliver Markham!"

I hesitate because she's got a point. It's not entirely a lie either, but it wasn't the whole truth. "Oliver Markham Graeme," I say. "Markham is a family name. I knew...I knew it would be enough for anyone to locate me, coupled with my birthday and picture, if that alleviates any retroactive safety concerns of yours."

"Graeme," she mumbles. "You're Professor Graeme. But...but you're not old at all." Her cheeks go pink in the most tempting way, and then I notice—oh Christ—her nipples have pulled tight under the criminally thin fabric of her camisole.

Fuck. How dare she be so delicious now? When I'm so furious with her?

She drops the poker, and it bounces off a pile of books. "But you have slippers and everything," she whispers.

Why is she so fixated on my damn slippers? And how does she know I even have them unless she's been in my bedroom?

She's been in my bedroom.

A desperate, lust-filled rage floods me anew. "Tell me one thing," I demand. "Did you really not know? Did you really not know it was me?"

She shakes her head vehemently. "That was the whole plan," she says, gesturing in front of her as if *the plan* is something she can trace the shape of. "That's why it had to be London. It had to be a stranger. I wanted to get rid of it and then go on with my life."

I study her. Years of fibbing and malingering students have given me a keen ability to detect the truth, and there's nothing but honesty glowing from her blue eyes and flushed cheeks.

She didn't know.

A realization comes, jagged with relief and something that's too close to disappointment. "You should leave."

"Right," she says, smoothing down her hair. Her tits move under her camisole with mouthwatering heaviness. "I should go to bed, and then we'll discuss this after we've had some sleep."

"No," I interrupt. "I mean you should *leave*. Go back home."

I'm not prepared for the sudden hurt and unhappiness that floods her face. "Oliver," she says.

"It's Professor Graeme."

"Professor," she says. "Please."

The proximity of those two words together, coming out of a mouth like hers, lances heat right to my groin.

Professor, please.

Fuck.

"I really, really want this," she continues. "Not just for the work, although it will be invaluable to have on my résumé, but to have a summer that's somewhere new and different. If you send me home, I'll just be bored and alone with nothing to do, and I promise to be good if you let me stay. I'll be so, so good, Professor. Please."

I have to swallow.

Remember again that I'm a man and not a monster. "It's impossible, Zandy. Surely you see that. It's wildly inappropriate for us to work together now."

Her tongue peeps out to wet her lower lip. "I won't be inappropriate," she whispers. "I promise."

Does she not understand? She is inappropriate without even trying. Her earnestness. Her extravagant body. Everything about Zandy Lynch is fiercely unseemly, and it makes me crave very unseemly things. I can't have her in this house—her spiced and flowery scent in my nose, her dark hair catching the sunlight in my study—and not want to bend her over a desk. Not want her on her knees with her mouth open and those blue eyes trained up at me as she waits for the crumbs of my approval.

And I've vowed not to be that man anymore. Whatever happened in London be damned, I'll control myself starting now.

I ignore the tear-shine in her eyes when I say, "You'll leave tomorrow. We'll make the arrangements in the morning."

I mean to leave her there, with the finality of my decision hanging around her, but I have to stop. I don't turn to look at her. I simply make sure she hears me. "I don't like how you talk about your virginity like it's a burden. Something you had to coax a stranger into doing away with. It was a gift to me."

Then I leave her among the books and the papers, and when I reach my bedroom, I pull out my cock with embarrassingly frantic hands and stroke myself, thinking of those tits under her camisole. And after I come all over my fist and clean up, I kick my slippers under my bed with a growl, crawl into bed, and lie awake for untold hours, Zandy Lynch haunting my thoughts like a spirit haunts a house.

♦ ♦ ♦ ♦

I barely sleep. And around five, when the sun is beginning to paint the sky on the other side of my little valley, I climb out of bed. Frustrated and hard, even after two more rounds with my fist. Quiet rounds, so that she wouldn't hear, although I almost wanted her to. I wanted her to creep by the door and listen to what she did to me. I wanted her to push her way in as boldly as she pushed her way into my night three days ago and demand to be fucked.

Beg to be fucked.

Promise to be her professor's good girl.

Of course it didn't happen, and I came into a T-shirt like a fucking adolescent, furious all the while. I'd done so well after Rosie—so well for *years*—and now here's Zandy Lynch with her mouth just made for my cock, with her backside just begging to be spanked.

Grumbling, I fish out my slippers from under the bed, yank some drawstring pants up over my hips, and pull on a clean T-shirt. If I can't sleep, I may as well work.

Beatrix joins me as I make a cup of tea and set out some of the latest texts I've been reading, along with my notebook and pen. She curls up on the table next to my notebook, oblivious to how many times I nudge at her to make writing room for my hand, and together we work until the kitchen slowly fills with light and the sun decides to peer directly into my house. I flip over the latest sheet of what I've been reading—a selection from a Victorian ladies' magazine—and move it to the edge of my workspace, which happens to be a nearly perfect square of sunlight coming in through the window.

"You really shouldn't expose it to the light like that," comes a voice from behind me, and it takes everything I have not to flinch at the sudden intrusion.

Zandy appears at the edge of my vision, her body in some kind of knit dress that looks nearly pornographic on her curves, her hair woven into a long, messy braid—the kind of braid that makes a man think of pulling on it. Her mouth is curved into a small smile as she sits at the kitchen table, but there's a flat sheen of defeat in her eyes.

I look away from her and rub at my chest again. "I suppose next you'll chide me for not using gloves."

"Actually, you shouldn't use gloves with paper," she says. "The fibers of the glove might catch on the document, and it's also important to have a feel for the page itself as you handle it. It's a delicate thing, handling something that rare, and you need every tiny, minute sensation to help you feel for whether it's brittle or supple. Whether it might break or bend."

I'm hard.

From her talking about paper.

"Duly noted," I say shortly, hoping she doesn't see how she's affected me. I tug the page out of the sunlight. A moment passes, when I pretend to go back to my reading and ignore her—as if I could ignore her. My body definitely can't.

She endures the silence for an admirably long time. And then, "Are you really going to send me home?"

She asks it in a soft voice, and when I look up, I see that defeat in her gaze again. I can't say why it bothers me, only that it does. Only that in the bizarre and short circumstances of our acquaintance, I've come to expect that blue gaze to bubble over with confidence and eager energy.

I set my pen down and run a hand over my face. "You have to see why it's impossible."

"But I don't. I already told you I'd be good. I'd be better—"

"Your father sent you to me with the tacit implication that I'd keep you reasonably safe during your stay. Do you honestly think he'd be comfortable with you staying in my house if he knew what happened in London?"

"I'm twenty-two," Zandy insists, leaning forward. "He knows I'm an adult. And besides, it was one time. *One time.* And we didn't know who the other really was. It's an outlier, not even a real data point, and it should be thrown out."

I scowl at her. I scowl because there's a part of her argument that's logical and because I don't even care about the parts that aren't. As much as I know she needs to go, as much as I want her to go—dammit, *I do*—my thoughts keep crowding with plans and ideas and all the moments we'd have together if she stayed.

"And," she says, sensing my weakness and gaining momentum now, "you really do need someone to fix this mess of yours."

"It's not a mess," I say coldly, but we both know I'm lying. Mess is possibly the kindest word for it.

"I can organize it, index it all, and store it safely. And you won't even know I'm in the room."

I have the vision of Zandy brushing sweaty tendrils of hair off her forehead as she carries books around, bending over often. Scratching away at her desk like a good little girl.

I have to swallow again.

"Please, Professor?" she asks, leaning forward so much now that her breasts press against the table. But that's not what I chiefly notice this time. No, it's her eyes, sparkling like sunlight dancing off ocean waves, even as she braces herself for my rejection.

I abruptly want that look out of her eyes. I want to see her eyes as they were that night we spent together, awed and worshipful and happy. That's the only reason I can think of for why I say it.

"Fine."

"Fine?" Her entire face lights up, a happy flush high on her cheeks and her eyes like blue fires. She looks like she wants to kiss me.

I wonder how I look.

"Yes. Fine. You can stay."

CHAPTER SEVEN

ZANDY

Oliver stands up, the sunlight catching on the waves of his hair. He impatiently shakes it out of his eyes, just as he did earlier when I stood behind him and watched him work. He'd been too absorbed to hear me as I walked in, too absorbed to notice me staring at his long fingers as they gripped his pen and made notes in an endearingly untidy scrawl. His too-pale skin and disheveled hair make sense to me now, fitted into the context of his work. He's an obsessed scholar, subsumed by his projects, and it's easy to see how the everyday details of life have become unimportant. My father is the same way, and so are most of his friends. They'd forget to eat if someone didn't remind them.

"I'm going to change," Oliver says in that short, clipped way of his, "and then I'll be back downstairs and we can begin." He still doesn't sound pleased, but I'm so relieved I get to stay that I ignore his grouchiness.

"Is there anything I can do while you get ready? Make you some coffee?" I think for a minute, remembering where I'm at. "Tea?"

He narrows his eyes. "Just don't touch anything while I'm not around."

"Whatever you say," I reply, fast enough that it nearly sounds sarcastic. "Professor," I add, hoping that will ameliorate any unintentional offense.

His eyes darken at my last word, and he stalks from the room as if I've enraged him.

I sigh the moment I think it's safe. While I'm used to grumpy scholars, Oliver has to be the grumpiest I've ever encountered. Well, not grumpy, exactly. *Cold* is a better word. Glacial, even.

Unfeeling.

Stony.

I stand up and stretch, deciding *don't touch anything* surely doesn't extend to coffee or tea and needing the familiar act to steady myself, because holy fuck, Oliver Markham is Professor Graeme.

The man I'm spending the summer with is the man who ended my virginity, and if I was worried about my ability to be wise and sophisticated about this before, it's nothing compared to now.

Because even with as cool and distant as he is, I still yearn for his touch. Even with his gaze flashing displeasure, I crave the trace of it over my body. Even in its cruelty, his perfect mouth begs for my own mouth, my fingertips. And even covered with a T-shirt and loose pants, his leanly muscled body calls to mine, bringing me memories of how he looked moving between my legs, memories of how taut and rigid he went as he filled my pussy with his own ecstasy.

I take a deep, steadying breath, trying to stop my body's response to the visions of that night, to the presence of him in the house. I can't work next to him like this, all wet and nipples hard, not when I need to prove to him how professional I can be. I'll save it for bedtime, when I'm alone in the dark, one hand clapped over my own mouth so he can't hear me come.

Like I did last night.

Oliver doesn't have any coffee, so I decide to make a cup of tea. I find a mug, fill it with water, and pop it in the microwave for a couple of minutes. When it's done, I carefully take it out, and I'm about to drop in the bag when Oliver says in a horrified voice, "What on earth are you doing?"

I whirl to see him looking unfairly sexy in a thin sweater and belted trousers that hang low on his narrow hips. He's leaning against the kitchen doorway, his arms crossed and a frown on that sharp-edged mouth.

"I'm making tea?" I say, the last part lifting up like a question because I'm feeling suddenly unsure. Maybe I grabbed his favorite mug, or maybe I'm using some precious store of teabags that visitors aren't allowed to touch—or maybe visitors aren't allowed to touch anything at all, and he's provoked that I didn't listen to his edict about touching things.

"That's not how you make tea," he says. "You use the *kettle* for tea, not the microwave as barbarians do."

The disgust in his voice is so pronounced that I can't help but giggle. This only deepens his frown.

"We have work to do," he bites out. "Follow me. Bring that cup of atrocity if you must."

I do bring my cup of atrocity, following him down the hall

and trying very hard not to notice how his ass and hips look in his pants—tight and trim. Powerful in a subtle, spare way. Powerful in the kind of way that makes a girl think of how they'd feel under her hands. How they'd look bunching and flexing between her thighs.

I give a little shiver. *Down, girl.*

I've got to be good today. I've got to prove that he doesn't need to send me home.

The cat winds between our feet as we walk into the study, plopping down on the first pile of papers she sees, and I set my mug on my desk and wait for Oliver to give me instructions.

He stands behind his own desk now, gazing at me with a haughty expression. "You'll do as I say in here," he says flatly. "That's without question. Understood?"

"Understood."

His hands are flexing by his sides as he looks at me, and for a moment, all I can remember is the way they felt as he spanked me. One palm setting fire to my skin as the other hand held me steady over his lap.

I have to press my legs together at the sudden throb my clit gives at the memory. Who would have thought I'd like being spanked so much? So much that not only had I become a wet, squirming mess at the time, but that I longed for it again?

He swallows, and I realize that his beautiful eyes are no longer on my face but on my body. On the place where I'm pressing my thighs together.

"Sit," he commands hoarsely. "Get something to take notes with."

I sit, finding a notepad and a pen that have been shoved

into one of the drawers. "Ready when you are, Professor," I say, and he makes a noise, tearing his eyes away from where I sit with my legs crossed and pen poised in the air.

He sits as well, keeping his gaze away from me. "I'm writing a book about Victorian courtship narratives," he says to the William Holman Hunt painting on his wall. "Not necessarily the rituals themselves but the morality tales given to young people in order to illustrate how they *should* behave. As well as the satirical tales that illustrate how they *did* behave."

"And how did they behave?" I ask as I write.

"As youth everywhere and in every time behaves," he says grimly. "Improperly."

I look up at him with a smile. He doesn't smile back, glancing away from me as soon as our eyes meet. "Surely that's kind of heartwarming," I say. "Kind of fun? To think even Victorians couldn't help being naughty?"

Oliver presses his eyes closed. "I think," he says slowly, "it proves that we never learn from the mistakes of the past."

There's a deep bitterness in his words that takes me by surprise; whatever he's thinking of at the moment, it's viciously unhappy. It has teeth, and it's chewing at his mind—I can see it playing out across his beautiful face.

And then he opens his eyes with a long inhale, speaking to the painting once more. "I've only been through a third of the things I've collected, perhaps less, and so as part of any organization scheme, we need to index if I've seen it before."

"Of course," I say, jotting that down. "What else do you need? Digitization?"

He makes a face—it's very similar to the face he made at

my cup of tea. "I prefer paper."

"Victorian paper is very cheap and very acidic," I inform him. "Even in the best of conditions, which..." I trail off meaningfully, tilting my head at the room of decaying paper sitting in the sunlight.

"And?" Oliver prompts testily.

"And some of these paper works are not going to be around much longer. By the time you get to them, they may crumble in your hands. Digitizing what you can isn't just helpful for your research, it's the responsible thing to do as potentially the sole owner of some of these texts."

He gives a put-upon sigh. "If you think it necessary...then I suppose."

"I'll only mark the most at-risk items for photographing or scanning," I promise. I make a few more notes and give the room an assessing look. "We'll need to order some archival supplies—is there room in the budget for that?"

"The budget," he echoes, sounding puzzled.

"Dad said you were working with grant money."

"Oh yes, the grant." He gives a shrug that conveys something close to discomfort, and I watch curiously, as I've never seen him truly uncomfortable before—only annoyed. "Money is not a concern," he says, and he actually looks embarrassed by this. Maybe it was an exceptionally large grant and he feels strange about accepting it? Who knows.

"Okay, then," I say, standing up. "Shall we get started?"

An imperious look. "You shall get started. *I* shall work."

"Yes, Professor." I say it perhaps too mockingly, earning myself a glare, and I scuttle over to the far corner of the room and get to work before he scolds me again.

It becomes clear that Oliver's system, if that word can even be used, has been to stack the most promising texts closest to his desk and the least promising in the corners and along the far wall. I work steadily through the morning, building up a light sweat as I shift through stacks of material, trying to get a handle on what I'll need to know to build a comprehensive database for Oliver.

Several times I peek up over my work to watch him at his desk, unable to stop myself from staring at the chiseled jaw flexing in concentration and the long eyelashes sweeping against his cheeks as he studies his papers and types on his laptop.

It should be illegal for a man to be that handsome *and* English. It just isn't fair.

I suspect he doesn't want to be bothered, so around lunchtime I wander into his kitchen and make us simple sandwiches, bringing his plate back and wordlessly setting it at the edge of his desk. He reaches for the food automatically, eyes pinned to his laptop screen, and it isn't until he's finished his sandwich that he seems to realize he's eaten it at all.

"Thank you," he says after a minute, and I notice that his voice has thawed the tiniest bit. Not much. But a bit. I'm already back to work, and I look up to see him staring at me with an expression I can't decipher.

"You're welcome, Professor," I say, and he grunts in response. I take it as progress and fight a smile as I lean back down to my stacks of books.

♦ ♦ ♦ ♦

The day passes much the same as this. I finally get my laptop from my room and start on the database. Oliver sighs a lot at the frequent tapping of my keyboard, but when I offer to go work in the kitchen, he merely scowls and mutters, "Stay."

So I stay.

Around six, I bring up the subject of dinner and ask if he'd like me to make it. He seems to fight some inner war with himself. "I'll order takeaway," he says, which is how we end up eating delicious Indian food at the kitchen table with his cat complaining loudly at our feet.

"How did the writing go today?" I ask innocently enough, and he stabs at his butter chicken with a fierce frown.

"You should know better than to ask any writer that question."

"So it went well?"

He directs the frown at me. "You're teasing me." He says it incredulously, as if no one has ever dared do it before. In fact, I'm suddenly quite certain no one ever has dared to tease him before this. He's very un-teasable, with that haughty face and icy gaze. But I'm feeling energetic and playful from my own productive day, and it's so very hard not to provoke him when he makes such handsome provoked faces.

"I won't tease you any more if it hurts your feelings," I poke.

He glares at me. "It doesn't hurt my feelings."

"You seem a little hurt."

"I'm not hurt."

"In fact, I think I need to make it up to you," I banter back. "Maybe you can make me write an essay on my bad behavior."

His pupils dilate at the same instant that my own words filter back through my mind, along with their subtext. Which is punishment.

Which of course makes me think of the night we were together, which of course makes me want to be bent over that strong knee again. And with the way Oliver's fingers are clenched around his fork, I wonder if he's wanting the same thing.

"Excuse me," he says abruptly, standing up and setting his dishes by the sink. He leaves to go to his study, and I hear the door close firmly behind him. The message is clear.

Do not follow.

Feeling a little flushed from my body's immediate response to the idea of punishment from Oliver, I clean up after dinner and go upstairs. I mean to read for a while or maybe watch a movie on my tablet, but by the time I shower and get in bed, I'm more worked up than ever. I make sure my door is locked, and then I quietly climb into bed. I reach into my panties and let my mind fill with everything Oliver—his ferocious hands and his wicked mouth and his cock so heavy and so thick with wanting me.

It doesn't take long, the climax, because it's been building all day. All day like a slow fire inside me, and at the first touch of my hand, my body is already quivering and tense, ready to snap like a rubber band. The orgasm is fast and furious and ultimately unsatisfying, and when I come down from it, I come down with an itchy feeling of disappointment.

Of unabated longing.

And then as I sigh and pull my hand away from myself, I hear it—the creak of a floorboard outside my room. I go completely still, flooded with embarrassment and something else that's harder to name.

Anticipation?

Hope?

Do I want Oliver to kick down the door, pin me to the bed, and finally go all professor on me?

Yes. Yes, I do.

God, I want it more than anything.

The floorboard creaks again, and I can't breathe. I can't move. I'm ready for him to force his way in here and relieve the still-aching need deep in my core.

But he doesn't.

Hushed silence fills the corners and crevices of the room, and I'm left alone. Empty. Unfulfilled.

Sleep takes a long time to find me after that.

♦ ♦ ♦ ♦

A week goes by like this. During the day, Oliver is uncommunicative and distant. I work and he works, and I steal glimpses of him working, his light-brown hair burnished in a near-gold by the June sunlight and his jaw ticking in that particular way of his as he thinks. I feed him lunch, which he barely notices, and then at some point I tentatively bring up dinner, which is almost always some kind of carryout and also an excuse for him to jab angrily at his food until he finds a reason to leave the table.

And then I go up to my room and read or work until I can't stand it anymore, and I rub myself to climax. I never do hear that floorboard again, but every single time I hope I do.

I hope Oliver comes in and claims me. I want it more than I want anything, even more than I wanted to stay. Or maybe I wanted to stay because I wanted him to claim me more than anything. *So much for being sophisticated, Zandy.*

By my seventh day, the air in the study is thick with tension.

The sun is hot through the window, and I'm a very dismayed American when I realize that a box fan is the closest thing Oliver has to air conditioning. We crack open the windows and angle the fan so it doesn't blow century-old paper everywhere, but it barely helps. Even the cat escapes the house with a cantankerous meow, jumping out the open window and loping into the back garden in search of shade.

My sleeveless dress is too hot, and I'm tugging constantly at the neckline, feeling warm and flushed even with my hair fastened up on top of my head. I'm jealous of the cat, jealous of her shade, but all of my work is here in the study, and I can't leave either my work or Professor Grouch, who is even grouchier than usual today.

The second time I trip over a stack of books, making a ton of mess and noise, Oliver slams his laptop shut. "You," he says darkly.

Just that.

Just *you.*

And then he glares at me.

"I'm sorry," I say. "It's just messy and hot and...what is it?"

"Do you even care that you're making it impossible for me to work?"

Normally, I find his arrogant coolness sexy or amusing, but not today. It's too hot for one thing, and I'm eyeballs deep in fixing *his* mess, and so I snap back, "Not in the slightest."

I know instantly that I've fucked up. Oliver is a man of little patience, and the kind of lippy insolence I just displayed is absolutely one of his pet peeves. I feel a quick dart of fear that I've just managed to get myself fired.

Get myself sent home.

Shit.

Oliver's face could be cut from stone right now, and his words are made of ice when he finally speaks. "Come here."

"Oliver—"

"You call me professor in here or nothing at all," he interrupts coolly.

"Professor—"

"Come. *Here.*"

With some trepidation, I straighten my dress and walk toward him, bracing myself for the inevitable words. *You're fired. Get out of my sight.* And I hate the way tears burn at the back of my eyes, the way my throat balls up, because it's stupid that I have grown so attached in such a short amount of time. Not just to this beautiful cottage in this beautiful place but to *him*, the most beautiful thing of all. If I had to leave him, I wouldn't be able to bear the disappointment.

Disappointment. What a stupid word.

I'd be heartbroken.

Oliver regards me from across his desk, his arms folded

over his chest, his mouth pressed in a flat line. "Come *here*," he repeats, and I realize what he wants. He wants me close to him, on the other side of his desk.

My heartbeat kicks up a thousand paces. My mouth goes dry. He wants me close so that there's no mistaking his angry dismissal. He wants me close so that he can make it very, very clear that I have to leave. And maybe I deserve it. Not for knocking over books but because I haven't been a very good girl at all this week, what with all the silent, pining looks I've been throwing his way and the equally silent masturbating in his guest bed.

Tears threaten to spill out of my eyes, and crazy promises threaten to spill out of my mouth: that I really will be good this time, that I'll be the best assistant a professor could have, that I'll happily endure all of his moods and cutting remarks if only he'd let me stay close to him.

But I swallow both the tears and the words. I need to keep my dignity, I know at least that much about myself. That when I'm back home in my tiny apartment, curled around an empty bottle of wine, I'll be able to hold on to the memory of me being composed and resilient, to the knowledge that I didn't humiliate myself.

As I walk around the desk, Oliver pushes his chair back as if he'll stand, but he stays seated, keeping his body angled to the front. I take a deep breath, willing myself to be as cool and untouchable as he is, waiting for him to say the words that will send me home.

But those aren't the words he says.

"Red means stop," he tells me, and then I'm seized and

thrown over his lap.

Blood rushes to my head as my hands find the floor in pure instinct, and his hands easily catch and arrange me, one of his long legs hooking over mine when they kick up in the air.

And I'm wet.

Instantly, shamefully wet.

It's like all the silent orgasms and all the daylight fantasies and muffled desire, they are all concentrated into longing for this one thing, this one act. I don't need a kiss or a murmured compliment—I need *this*. To be bent over Oliver's knee like a disobedient schoolgirl.

And *he* needs it too. That much is clear from the way his hands tremble as they shape over my backside, smoothing over the fabric of my dress with a slowness that feels very much like desperation in disguise. A thick shape nudges into my hip, solid and blunt, and the tangible proof that he wants me is enough to make me whimper.

The whole thing is enough to make me whimper.

He's not going to be hearing any safe words out of my mouth. Not today.

"You make it impossible for me to work," he breathes. "You make it impossible to concentrate. To eat. To sleep."

"Because I made a mess?" I ask tremulously.

His hand slips under the hem of my dress and palms my backside. "Because you made a mess," he says in a growl, squeezing my ass hard enough for me to yelp. "And because you distract me with your dresses and your fucking hair and your fucking watch." He flips the skirt of the dress up over my waist, baring my ass and thighs to the warm air of the room.

"What are these?" he asks dangerously, a finger tracing along the lacy edge of my panties.

"Um, underwear," I answer, my face burning and my core clenching. I want so very badly for him to stroke along my center, to slip a finger inside of the lace and rub me where I'm swollen and wet, but he doesn't. He just continues with that maddening tease.

"These are the kinds of things bad girls wear," he says sternly. "Are you a bad girl?"

"Yes," I exhale. "Yes, I am."

The first spank. I squeal, my body arching away from the force, but there's nowhere to go, nowhere to be except against his hot, firm body.

"You know what else makes it impossible?" he asks.

"What?" I manage.

"Listening to you come on your own hand, night after night."

I suck in a guilty breath, grateful he can't see my face. "I— that's not—I mean—"

"Don't lie to me, Miss Lynch."

Not Zandy.

Not even Amanda.

Miss Lynch, like I'm a misbehaving student of his. The thought turns me on beyond all belief, and I squirm in his lap. "I didn't mean to—"

"You're lying," he accuses. "You think I don't know what you do at night, dirty girl? You think I don't know how you slip your fingers between your legs and wish it were my fingers? My mouth? My cock?"

I'm so far gone with lust at this point that all I can do is moan.

"Did you do it to drive me mad? Hmm?" Another spank. "Did you do it hoping I would break down the door and fuck you like your fingers couldn't?"

"Yes," I whisper as another spank lands hard. "Yes, I wanted that."

"Naughty girl," he admonishes. "Very naughty girl." Several more rain down on my backside, and I am past struggling now, past anything but the need for friction against my clit, the need to be filled deep inside.

"Please," I beg wildly. My hair is tumbling down around my face, and my nose is starting to run, and it feels like I've been spanked within an inch of my life, and I need *something*, something only he can give me. "Please, Oliver."

He gives me an almighty spank. "Try again."

"*Please, Professor.*"

"Much better," he rumbles, and then his fingers are right where I need him, pressing against the fabric covering my pussy. He tugs the panties aside, studying his prize for a long moment before fingering me in rough exploration. He makes a noise of approval at what he finds.

"So wet," he says with crude pleasure. "So wet for me."

His hand grips my hair and turns my head so I can look at him—his other hand keeps working at my sopping-wet pussy, teasing my entrance and working inside my channel so slowly that my toes curl.

"What do you want, Miss Lynch?" he asks, and he's as scornfully proud as ever, but there's something in the way he asks and in the way his hand pauses inside me...

He's waiting for me to carry this kinky game of his further. He's waiting for me to choose. And it's not even a choice. It hasn't been a choice since I clung to him in the London rain.

I will never choose *red*.

"I want to be your good girl, Professor Graeme. Please let me be your good girl again."

CHAPTER EIGHT

OLIVER

I knew this morning that I was near my breaking point.

All week it's been building, stoked by every fire imaginable. Her adorable and distracting habit of running the top of her pen over her lip as she worked. The thoughtful feeding and bringing of fresh mugs of tea, once she figured out the kettle. The unknowing way she flashed me her panties as she crawled on all fours around my office, shifting through stacks of research.

And at night...*fuck*.

It was purely an accident the first time. I was passing down the hallway to get a glass of water when I heard her. It was only a quiet *mmm* of feminine relief, but it went through me like an electric shock. I froze to the spot, instantly picking up on the rustle of sheets and the quickening of breath and—God have mercy on my soul—a sound that could be nothing other than a slender finger moving through a wet pussy.

I listened, hard and throbbing, until the very end with her sweet gasp of pleasure, and then I stole back to my room to toss off fast and vicious, coming so quickly that I could barely catch my breath.

I've repeated the voyeurism every night since.

How could I not?

I burned with wanting her, I ached with being so near and yet holding myself back, and by today, I was near mad with it. Her lewd curves and even lewder mouth, both combined with those still-innocent eyes. And then she had to go and put her hair up, with only a few damp tendrils escaping, as if to taunt me by caressing all the places along her neck and shoulders that I could not.

I didn't care that she knocked over a stack of books. I *cared* that she made me a madman. A wild thing, a beast, a hunter.

A monster.

I cared that I wanted her beyond all sense and propriety, and I cared that she was too fucking smart and helpful for me to find any fault with.

I cared, in other words, that she was perfect, and that by being perfect, she made me the most imperfect version of myself.

So as I hold her over my lap, one hand twisted in that luscious hair and the other still wet from her cunt, I ask her one last time. "Are you sure you want to be my good girl? It will take a lot of work."

She pulls her plump lower lip between her teeth. "Red means stop, right? So I say *red* when I need a time-out?"

"That's correct, Miss Lynch."

She blinks up at me. "Then that's all I need to know. Do what you like with me, Professor."

Christ, but she's dangerous. Some kind of siren sent to lure me off my path. I push her to her knees in front of me, spreading my legs on either side of her, enjoying the view of her big blue eyes all sultry as she looks up at me. I enjoy it almost as much as I enjoyed the glowing skin of her ass. Almost as much as examining the tight entrance to her body, all pink and wet, and remembering how unthinkably tight she'd been around my penis that night. How I had to wedge my way in.

Hell, I enjoy it all. I drink it all in like a man who hasn't tasted a drop of water in years.

"You've made me hard, like a bad girl," I drawl, loving how her eyes widen at the word *hard.* "And a good girl would fix it."

"Fix..." she asks, and then her cheeks go very pink. "*Oh.*"

"Yes. Take it out, Miss Lynch. I'm getting impatient."

Her hands are nervous and unpracticed as she works my belt open. "I've never..." Her voice comes out in a faltering murmur that's unlike her usual confident alto. She clears her throat. "I've never done this."

"Then just do as I say," I inform her.

She nods, squaring her shoulders a bit, and sets her attention to the task, like any good student would. There's something deeply erotic about her inexperience, something that makes it more than the playacting this kind of roleplay usually is.

A part of this is real—so real that it might be wrong—and I can't bring myself to stop it. I let the wrongness of it wash over me, opening to it, letting it inside a cold, sleeping heart that's been dead to real pleasure for far too long.

I hiss as her hands seek me out, drawing my naked and ruddy flesh into the air.

She stares at it with just as much awe and panic and

excitement as she did that night in London—as if she can't wait to have me inside her even as she knows I'll be too big—and that makes me want to pound my chest like a caveman. Makes me want to pull her up onto the chair and thrust into her wet opening. I want her impaled on me. I want her writhing from the stretch of me. I want her coming so hard her body tries to curl into a ball because she can't stand it, she just can't stand it.

But for now, I settle for this: "Put your mouth there, Miss Lynch."

Her eyelashes flutter as she looks up at me. "But what if I'm not any good at it?"

Frankly, it's a miracle I haven't erupted all over her already, but I don't break character to tell her that. "Then you'll have to practice. Best to start now."

The lower lip gets bitten, and one eyebrow arches slightly in a movement I know means she's deep in thought. And then she leans forward and presses a chaste kiss to the underside of my cock.

"Like that?" she asks, peering up at me. Her mouth is still close enough to my flesh that I feel the sweet puffs of her breath.

My belly clenches. "Almost, Miss Lynch. Use your tongue. Lick me."

"Lick," she murmurs to herself. "I can do that." And she does, setting that plush mouth to me once again, this time parting her lips, allowing her tongue to slip out.

The second it touches me, I let out a ragged breath; it's heaven, pure heaven, and the look she gives me is nothing short of vixenish—which, despite everything, despite how lurid and depraved this moment is, almost makes me smile with a grudging kind of respect. I can say many things about Zandy Lynch, and most of them are grievances—that she's too bold, too eager, too *happy*—but those are also the same things I can't ever imagine changing about her. They are the same things that reassure me that, while I might be a monster, I'm still a monster with a conscience, because the girl between my legs knows exactly what she's doing. She'll survive this.

Even if I don't.

She licks me again, less tentative this time and more certain, a long steady motion that has my blood heating and freezing in fitful starts. And then her natural eagerness spills over and she starts licking at my crown as if it's a lollipop, like she can't get enough of it. I thread my hands through her hair, but I don't push her down. Not yet. I simply flex and twist my fingers in the silky strands and guide her mouth to where I need it. From my taut, swollen tip to the turgid base, from the root to the velvety underside, rewarding her with my groans whenever she does well.

"Suck it," I say hoarsely. "Put it in your mouth and suck."

She does.

The flood of heat and soft wet is almost too much, and I'm gritting my teeth against the urge to come. "God, you suck me so good," I groan, my head falling back against my chair. I keep my hands in her hair, pushing her down just far enough to get that squeeze at the head of my prick. "Fuck."

I look down at her, and she's a vision like this, her dark hair tumbling everywhere around my hands and her perfect mouth wrapped around my cock. Her cheeks are hollowed and her eyes are wet and blue, and I think I could look at this for the rest of my life. Except there's something I want to see more.

"On your feet," I tell her, wincing as her hot mouth leaves my cock to throb wet and alone in the air of the room. I stand as she stands, and then I bend her over the desk, ignoring the papers and notes that go flying as I do.

"Stay here," I command, and I go up to my bedroom to find a condom. The box in my end table is depressingly old, and it would be funny to think that I've seen more sex in the past week than I have in the past three years if it weren't so painfully true. I find myself taking the steps back downstairs faster than I should, not only excited to get back down to Zandy and her willing body, but also crawling with this odd fear that I'd return to the study and find her gone. That she'd come to her senses and leave and take her forthright sweetness elsewhere.

The fear is astonishingly pervasive, and I find myself rubbing at the tight spot in my chest as I push open the study door.

And find her still stretched over my desk, like the good listener she is.

The relief at seeing her nearly makes me stumble, nearly makes me drunk, and I'm on her with a fast desperation I don't care to identify. I bend over her body, covering her with mine. We're both still fully clothed, still sweaty in the June heat, and it makes it dirtier somehow. Coarser.

Obscene.

"Oliver," she pleads, voice breaking, and I don't correct

her this time. The game is melting away—into what, though, I'm not certain.

"I know what you need, girl. Hold still."

I straighten up and roll on the condom as fast as I've ever done it in my life, peeling her panties off her skin and kicking them away. I cup her pussy in my hand with a hard, possessive grip, and she wriggles against it, trying to get the friction against her clit, and she's so wet, so fucking wet, that my palm comes back slicked with her.

I use that hand to stroke my swollen cock once, twice, before nudging the shiny latex tip at her small opening. I remind myself that this is only her second time being fucked, to take it easy on her, and it's with all the unraveling self-control left in me that I refrain from slamming into that tight cunt with one savage thrust.

I settle for two savage thrusts instead.

The thick, heavy crown stretches her, and I get to halfway in, holding her hips down as she whimpers and tosses underneath me. And then I shove the rest of the way in, wishing I could listen to her noises forever. Her long, low cry as I fully seat myself inside her. Her pants and mewls as I roll my hips to feel the wet silk of her around my root. And then her eye-rolling moan as I slide my hand around her hip and start massaging the swollen pearl of her clit.

She is amazing like this, bent over my desk like some kind of academic sacrifice, her sweet ass filling one hand while my other hand works her into a frenzy. Her hair is a tumbled mess, and her eyes, when they flutter back at me, are lost and dazed and adoring. And her body around mine, even through the condom, is everything—soft and hot and tight beyond belief. A spark of wonder kindles in my chest that she's letting a miserable bastard like me fuck her again. That she's still happy and willing to play any kind of game with me after how I've acted the past week.

Christ, what a gift.

The spark kindles into a real fire now, something possessive and primal and as certain as the sun and the wind and the sparkling river glinting behind me as I fuck her.

She's mine.

Maybe it's just for this moment, as she starts quivering and fluttering around my cock, or maybe it's only for today. But she's mine, and I want to roar my pleasure at the knowledge.

I want more of her. More of this. This raw fucking with my hips plowing into her spank-reddened bottom, this sweet clenching around my cock as she comes. And after my own release tears through me, filling the condom with hot and heavy spurts, I barely give her a minute to breathe. I tear off the condom, scoop her limp and sweaty into my arms, and carry her up to my bedroom.

♦ ♦ ♦ ♦

I'm ravenous tonight. Insatiable. Because, selfish man that I am, if I'm going to break my rules and break the trust I have with her father, then I may as well do it thoroughly.

And I am very, very thorough.

I peel off her clothes and explore every exposed contour of her with my mouth. I feast on those abundant tits like I've been fantasizing about, like I've been stroking myself to the thought of all week, and I turn her into a wriggling, gasping mess.

"I forgot," she breathes out, her eyes glowing in the fading light of my bedroom.

"You forgot what?"

"That your mouth could feel so good there," she whispers as I kiss and lick at the softly curved underside of her breast. "That it would make me want you so much again."

"Then let me make it so you remember forever."

I move my lips from the underside to her nipple, tugging gently at the straining tip with my teeth and then drawing it into my mouth for a long, swirling suck. She arches underneath me, a movement that matches us together down below, and before I can do anything about it, she's rubbing her empty pussy against me, lifting her hips and grinding against my hardness.

The feel of her wet and soft against my bare cock is like a nightmare and dream wrapped into one, and for the first time in years, I find I want to fuck a woman bare. I want to push into Zandy with nothing between us, and I want her to see how raw she makes me, how vulnerable. I want her to feel every inch of what she does to me. I want her to feel it when I come in her, marking her.

Mine.

And then I duck my head down to kiss along her stomach, terrified of my own thoughts, terrified she'll see them. Terrified she'll see them and she won't be scared and I won't be scared either and we'll do something regrettable.

There's a good reason I fuck with condoms every time. There's a good reason I fuck with condoms always.

I work my way down the gentle curves of her stomach and then over the rise of her pubic bone, kissing and licking all the way.

"Stop," she gasps. "I'm sweaty, and I should clean myself if you're going to do that again and—"

"Is this a *red* stop, or is this you trying to hide yourself from me?"

"It's not a red stop," she clarifies. She has no idea how tantalizing she looks like this, her head propped on a pillow, near-black waves of hair everywhere, her nipples standing to attention and her wet cunt spread before me. "But I have been sweaty all day—"

"I make the rules," I inform her in a clipped voice. "In this bed, I'm the professor and you're my student, and I'm going to taste you. And then I'm going to fuck you."

She wiggles a little, color in her cheeks. "But..."

"Those are the rules, Miss Lynch. You want to follow my rules, don't you? Be a good girl for me?"

God, how she responds to me when I talk to her like this. Like she was made to fit me. Her mouth parts, and her tongue licks out at her lower lip. Her eyes are huge, dark pools of needy blue when she answers, "Yes, Professor."

I make a noise of satisfaction and resume my kissing, using my hands to spread her wide so she's completely on display for me. That night in London, I'd been too impatient, too fast—years of celibacy chasing me down and making me weak, and when she broke open my control, she broke open all of it. The restraint. The time I normally took with a woman in bed.

Not now. Not tonight.

Tonight, I'm in full control, and I take my time staring at her, using my thumbs to make it so she hides nothing. There's no wet secret of hers that I don't want to taste and learn. There's no hollow of her body that I don't want to know my touch.

Mine.

I trace every fold with my tongue, I suckle on the firm berry of her clit until she's moaning, and then right before she comes, I sheathe my cock in latex and drive home, kissing her aggressive and deep with a mouth still wet from her pussy.

"Zandy," I grind out, my hips changing from slow rolls to heavy, fast thrusts. "Fuck, Zandy, you feel so fucking good."

She is lost to the drive of me between her legs, her head tossing. "It's too much, Oliver," she mumbles, her eyes closed. "I can't—it's too—"

She comes so hard she screams, and I feel it all around my cock, a grip so tight that it almost feels like she's trying to push me out. It's work to fuck through all that—the most delicious kind of work—and when I come, it feels like something rips open inside me. Something that's been held back for far too long. The throbs are so sudden and strong that I find myself slumping over her, unable to keep my own body upright as I fill the condom and something rearranges itself deep in my chest.

After I clean us up, she looks like she thinks she should leave, and I climb into bed and anchor her to me with one arm around her stomach, pulling her back to my chest and her perfect rump into my hips. My knees tuck behind her knees, and her long hair is everywhere like a sea of floral-smelling shadows.

"Oliver?" she asks after a moment.

"It's the oxytocin," I mumble against her neck, and that seems to settle her.

But it takes a long time for me to fall asleep, and the reason why is that I know something she doesn't.

It's not the oxytocin.

It's because I'm not ready to let her go.

CHAPTER NINE

ZANDY

I wake up sore between the legs and happy. The kind of happy that has no real reason to it. The kind of happy that suffuses your blood before you even open your eyes. And when I do finally open my eyes to summer sunshine and Oliver's neatly furnished room, I'm smiling.

Before I'm even all the way conscious, I know he's gone. But I'm not upset by it—I've noticed that he takes himself on punishingly long runs most mornings; and anyway, I'm glad I get to have this very, very girlish moment to myself. The moment where I roll over and smell the sheets and squeal inwardly to myself.

Oliver fucked me again.

And more than that—he's been wanting me as much as I've been wanting him. Every glimpse I stole of his eyes and aristocratic mouth, he was stealing similar glimpses of me. He was wanting me, craving me...listening to me finger myself night after night in vivid torment.

The thought makes me curl and blush with agony— agonized shame and agonized delight. To be caught doing such things is beyond humiliating, and yet to know that those same things aroused and haunted him fills me with a smug feminine pride. To know that the person you want wants you back?

It's like a pure life arrowing right through the middle of me. Like I'm entirely new. An entirely new Zandy—not one who's too much but one who's just the right amount.

Just right for a man like Oliver.

The thought makes me blush anew with how stupidly juvenile it is, with how many unspoken hopes are woven through it, and I push myself out of bed to get away from it. From the wanting more, from the wanting things that Oliver almost certainly won't want to give. *Sophisticated*—I still need to be sophisticated.

So I have my best sophisticated face on as I go downstairs after I shower and dress. I enter the kitchen looking the perfect mix of cool and sultry, prepared to have a cool and sultry breakfast and...

Oliver's not here.

Probably still on a run, I think, but I deflate a little bit. Which is dumb.

Why am I acting so dumb?

Chiding myself, I make a cup of tea with the kettle—see, I'm learning—and then decide to get to work. That will please him, I think, to come back and find me at my desk. Maybe it will please him enough to let me have his cock again...

But then I go into the study, and he's there, and his very presence reverberates through my bones like a gong's been struck. The bent head, still proud, still haughty, even craned over his work. The long, strong fingers and the carved swells of muscle pressing against his shirt as he breathes. Those eyelashes so long on his cheeks and the prismatic eyes themselves.

Eyes like I've never seen before I met him. Eyes as complicated and mysterious as the man they belong to.

I offer up a shy smile, my heart going a million miles a minute. I'm not sure what to say or what to do; all of this is completely uncharted for me. What do all these sophisticated, sexual women say to their lover-slash-bosses the morning after a tryst? *Hello?* Or perhaps *I'm wet just from looking at you. Can we do it again?*

But I can't be a sophisticated, sexual woman. I can only be Zandy. So I beam at him. "Hi," I say, giddily and somewhat lamely.

His mouth tugs down in a scowl. "Glad to see you're ready to start your work for the day."

"I didn't have my alarm set. I was..."

I was sleeping in bed with you, I want to say, but something stops me. His expression maybe, growing colder by the second, or the way his beautiful hands have gone still over his notebook.

Zandy that I am, I can't help but try again. "I slept so well, though. Last night was—"

"Last night was a mistake," he cuts me off. His voice is glacial, the words sharp enough to cut me with their corners. "And it won't happen again."

It takes too long for his words and their meaning to make sense in my mind, but once they do, I think I'd rather be drawn and quartered. I hate being so expressive, I *hate* it, and I hate that he can probably see the whip-cut of his words across my face. I duck my head so he can't see the shame, the hurt, the confusion.

Keep your dignity, Zandy, because it's the only comfort you'll be able to hang on to.

"Of course," I mumble, making my way over to my desk while trying not to let my tears fall. Trying not to let my mind race with the inevitable questions. The *whys*.

Am I not pretty enough? Thin enough? Cool enough? Was I bad in bed? Was it terrible sex and I had no idea because I'm so inexperienced? Or, oh God, what if I did something embarrassing in my sleep? Clung to him or drooled on him—or worse?

"You'll find a credit card on your desk," Oliver says to the side of my face once I'm seated. "For archival materials. Like I said before, there's no budget. Use what you need."

And those are the last words he says to me all morning.

My first jobs were as research assistants to my father's friends and of course to my father himself. Since the age of fourteen, I've spent summers and winter breaks running photocopies and flagging promising entries in annotated bibliographies. I'm used to working in rooms with humans so deep in thought that they forget I'm there. I'm used to working in silence.

This is different.

Every moment feels amplified, as if it's under a jeweler's glass, and every noise seems to quake through the room with geologic force. Even the burble of the river outside the open window is deafening. When I set down a handful of books and one drops on the floor, it's as if I've knocked the house over.

The air between us thrums with unhappy electricity, and it takes all morning for me to get to a point where I think I might not cry. How can he be so cold? How can he be so cruel?

And how—*how*—after all that I've scolded myself, could I have still gotten attached? Gotten all happy and hopeful and...I don't know...oxytocin-y?

Stupid, stupid, stupid.

I make him lunch as usual, and he eats it blindly as usual, and I hate how I still crave something from him in this moment—a compliment or a grunt of approval or anything. I hate how I still want to be his good girl. His teacher's pet.

♦ ♦ ♦ ♦

It's after lunch that I find the note.

It's in a pile of books under an ottoman, and despite the entire terrible morning, I can't help but give a cluck of librarian censure when I find them. The books have been shoved under the ottoman so haphazardly that a few pages are bent up, and one of the leather-bound volumes has a permanent dent in the spine. With a sigh, I gather the neglected babies to my chest and carry them over to my desk, where I'll catalog them for the database.

Which is when the note slips out.

I set the books on my desk and go back to retrieve it, painfully aware of how Oliver's eyes are not on me, aware of how studiously he ignores me. It burns, that rebuffing, burns like I'm being dipped in scalding water, and I know I have the red cheeks and swollen, tender heart to prove it. I try to ignore him back, pretend I don't care that the only man I've ever had sex with seems to hate me, and I scan over the piece of paper as I walk back to my desk.

Usually these loose bits of paper are receipts, if not from Oliver's purchase, then a previous owner's purchase from years back. Other times, it might be one of Oliver's own notes—a quick scrawl about why he bought the book or a more detailed write-up outlining the contents.

But instead of Oliver's messy, spiky hand, I see words in pretty and symmetrical loops, written in the kind of pen that leaves little flourishes at the end of every word.

Oliver,

You hardly ever remember the things you say in bed, but I do. I hope this is proof.

Your girl,

Rosie

My stomach twists, hiking itself up into my chest.

There's no mistaking the subtext to that note. There's no miscategorization. No shelving this on the wrong shelf. This Rosie, whoever she was, was Oliver's lover.

Or is still his lover, a quiet voice warns me. *How would you know?*

There's no date on the note, although it is the tiniest bit yellowed in one corner, which is to be expected if it's been stuck in a decaying book for any length of time. There's also no real way of telling which book the note fell out of, although I do notice that all the books from this pile deal with the subculture of Victorian erotica.

I flip through one of them and find my breath tangling around the twists in my stomach.

Lots of spanking in here. Lots of it. Drawings and photographs of women bent over, their petticoats all rucked up in heaps around their waists. Stories of wives and debutantes and schoolgirls getting disciplined, sometimes in very erotic circumstances and sometimes in simple morality tales.

What had Oliver told this Rosie in bed that prompted her to buy these things for him? Had he been talking about research as they nodded off toward sleep? Or had it been something more intimate? Did he play the same bedroom games with Rosie that he played with me?

Of course he did, that voice says. *You think he just decided to spank a stranger without ever having done it before?*

The whole thing—the professor and his good-girl game— is obviously Oliver's kink, and I might have been a virgin until just a week ago, but I was a very well-read virgin, and even I know that kinks don't just pop up overnight. Oliver must have done it with other women, which somehow nettles me more than thinking of him merely fucking another woman.

A bitter envy poisons my blood, and I walk over to his desk and drop the note onto the page he's reading.

"I found this," I say. "Looks important."

It's almost worth my own pain to see the flash of anguish in his eyes.

"Can I expect to find more things from Rosie?" I ask, too upset to care that I've finally succeeded in sounding very aloof and reserved right now. "Would you like me to set them aside or save them for you to look through?"

Oliver picks up the note, his jaw working to the side, his hands so still that he might be a statue of himself. Then he gives the note a vicious crumble and drops it in the small trash can by his desk. "Don't bother," he says shortly. "I don't want to see them."

And then he goes back to pretending I don't exist.

Perverse satisfaction buoys me for a moment or two. Whoever this Rosie is, she's not a lover of Oliver's any longer, it seems. But soon I'm weighed down with razor-sharp anguish again. At least he *talked* to Rosie in bed. I was only ravished within an inch of my life—not that I'm complaining—and then summarily scorned the next day...and I *am* complaining about that. He won't even look at me now, as if I'm beneath his attention, and yet I never feel like he's not aware of me. Of where I move and when I move, of how I sit and how I write. I just can't tell if his awareness is one of cold annoyance or of burning dislike. It can't be anything else.

It's the slowest afternoon of my life, and as it drones on, too warm and narrated by the drone of a bee that gets stuck inside the study and bumbles about while Beatrix watches, I begin to wonder if I can really do this for the rest of the summer. Can I sit in a room with a man I want, a man I gave my body to, and have him treat me like this?

No.

I'd rather be spanked every day, because an entire summer of Oliver treating me the way he's treated me today—that would be the real masochism.

After six o'clock rolls over, I close my laptop, coming to a decision. Dinner with Oliver would be an exercise in heartache and misery, and I can't bear it. I won't do it to myself.

If he wants to ignore me, fine. I'll make myself very easy to ignore.

♦ ♦ ♦ ♦

"May I sit here?" a warm voice asks, and I look up to see a very good-looking man in a button-down shirt and trousers standing next to me at the bar inside the Slaughtered Lamb pub.

"Of course," I say with a smile, and his face opens up with an answering grin.

"You're American."

I give a sheepish smile as I pat the stool next to me. "Take a seat, and I'll tell you all about it."

"That's an invitation no man can refuse." He chuckles, and there's a little bit of heat to his gaze as his eyes make a surreptitious flick over my body.

We both order drinks, and we start chatting—he does some type of accounting for a local quarrying company, and I explain why I'm spending my summer before grad school helping a scholar with research.

He seems charmed by me, and I can't help but wonder if this is how it would have happened if I'd made it to the Goose and Gander that night. If I'd met any other handsome Englishman, anyone other than Oliver. If it would've been as easy as I'd planned on it being—just two adults sharing a night together and then going their separate ways. Not whatever it is that Oliver and I have going on.

But at least I scored a point for my dignity tonight. I stood up and left the study as if I were simply going to get another mug of tea, and then I got my wallet and left the house, walking the short, pleasant route up to Bakewell and indulging in some Indian food before I decided to stop by the Slaughtered Lamb for a much-needed drink.

I hope Oliver enjoyed his dinner alone.

I hope he enjoys the rest of his summer alone, because I've made up my mind. I'm not going to stay. It stings and it rankles, having to give this up just because he's a colossal dick, but nothing's worth being this miserable. I'll go back tonight, announce that I'm leaving, and then tomorrow I'll be on my way home, away from him and his perfect eyes and his perfect mouth and his perfect everything that even now sets my body on fire just thinking about it.

"Have you been enjoying your stay?" Matthew the Quarry Guy says, and I feel a stab of guilt when I realize this isn't the first time Matthew's asked the question.

"I have been." I give him my renewed focus and another smile, which he seems to enjoy very much. "It's so beautiful here, so much more beautiful than I could have ever imagined."

"I'd be happy to show you around sometime," Matthew says, his voice going lower. "I'd hate for you to miss anything."

I'm about to tell him I appreciate it but I can't because an arrogant professor broke my heart and now I have to go home early, but I'm stopped by the sudden appearance of a man right behind Matthew.

A man with blue-green-brown eyes who's practically vibrating with rage.

"Oliver?" I ask as he takes my elbow.

"We're going home, Miss Lynch," Oliver says through clenched teeth, and oh, it's terrible, but hearing him call me Miss Lynch again makes me want to squirm in the best kind of way.

"May I help you?" Matthew asks, looking a bit alarmed for my sake, but Oliver cuts him a glare so ferocious that Matthew withers immediately, and I can't blame him.

"Only Miss Lynch can help me by coming home, which she's doing now, so any help from you is quite unnecessary," Oliver pronounces stonily. "If you'll excuse us."

I don't have to go with him. Not only could I struggle free if I wanted, but I think if I said *red*, he'd relinquish me right away. He'd let me go.

But I do go with him, flashing an apologetic smile at Matthew and letting Oliver guide me out the door of the pub, grateful that I've already paid my tab.

"What were you doing in there?" he demands the minute we're in the open air.

"Getting a drink."

"No. What were you doing with that man?"

I roll my eyes and start to pull away, but Oliver pins me against the outside wall of the pub, one hand on either side of my head and his body a shield of angry male in front of me.

"Were you going to let him kiss you?" he asks in a dangerous voice. "Were you going to let him fuck you?"

I want to say *yes*. I want to make Oliver angry and miserable, just as he's made me. I want to prove that I *am* sophisticated, that I do have dignity, and that I'm just as good at ignoring him as he is at ignoring me.

But like earlier today, I find I can only be Zandy. Honest, embarrassing Zandy.

"No," I admit, looking away.

"Fuck right, you weren't," Oliver growls. "He's not allowed to touch you."

"Why do you care?" I ask, searching his face. It's near-dusk, still light enough to be warm but dark enough for shadows to dance in his eyes. "You made it very clear today how you feel about me."

"That's what you think?"

"Yes," I shoot back hotly. "Yes, that's what I think. What else?"

"What else?" he breathes. "Not that you drive me mad? Not that I can't work, I can't focus, I can't even *think* when you're around me?"

We stare at each other, chests rising and falling with jagged breaths, our mouths nearly close enough to touch. To kiss.

My lips part and my eyes hood low, ready for him to lay waste to me with his skilled mouth and tongue. Ready for those hard, greedy kisses he delivered with such furious conviction for a man normally so cold.

He doesn't kiss me.

When I open my eyes all the way in confused disappointment, he's glaring at me like I've taken a match to his rare books. "We're going home *now*, Miss Lynch," he seethes, and I don't argue, because the minute I get back to his house, I'm packing my suitcase and *leaving*. I don't care if I sleep in some open-air train station. I am not staying.

I'm fuming as I climb into Oliver's car for the short ride to his house. Fuming and rehearsing my grand speech about leaving and how Oliver can go fuck himself. But when we pull up to the cottage and I get out of the car, Oliver meets me at my side, crowding me against the car door.

I expect more of his anger, or maybe that we'd go back to the cutting chill of earlier, but the man in front of me is neither angry nor cold. He's breathing hard, and there's something in his eyes that looks bruised and tender and young.

"I want you, Zandy, and I can't tell you how much that terrifies me."

Terrifies *him*? It's so hard to imagine this marble-cut man being terrified of anything, much less *me*.

"I don't understand."

He gives a bleak kind of laugh at that. "No. You wouldn't, because you're still happy and ready for the world. You're still unhurt. And I— I woke up this morning horrified at the thought that I may have stolen that from you."

I stare at him, beyond baffled. "What? By sleeping with me?"

He runs an agitated hand through his hair. "By sleeping with you and...all the other things."

The front garden is a dark haven of flowers and rich grass, lit only by the faint kitchen light coming out of the cottage, so it's hard to be sure—but I think I see color in Oliver's cheeks.

He's ashamed, I realize, and the thought is so bizarre to me, so foreign, that it takes a minute to absorb it. *He's ashamed of what he likes in bed.*

And abruptly, everything else—his behavior today, my

leaving—is set aside. Or, rather, filtered through the light of this new information.

"Oliver," I say, catching his eyes. "I *liked* what we did. Both times. It's sexy to me, and..." I search for the right word. "It's not any more complicated than that. I like it. Who cares if I like it because I was raised by professors or because I've worked for professors before or because I'm an incurable teacher's pet? It's fun, and I consented wholeheartedly. What more can there be to it than that?"

It's Oliver's turn to stare, and he's staring at me like he can't believe I'm real.

"What?" I ask, suddenly self-conscious.

"You," he says, like he said yesterday afternoon, except this time it's not dark or tortured. It's wondering.

Possessive.

The way he says *you* might as well be *mine*.

"Me?" I ask, and it's ridiculous, but I think I've been waiting to hear that word my entire life.

You.

"You," he repeats, and then his mouth slants over mine, hot and greedy, just like I've come to crave, and within an instant, I'm against the car, my legs around his waist and his arms crushing me tight to him. I have so much more to ask him, so much more to wonder about, but it's like everything shrinks to the points of contact between us: his mouth so searingly thorough and his lean hips between my thighs and his wide hands splayed over my ass. And where his erection pushes, thick and heavy, between my legs.

"Professor," I whimper into his mouth, and he shudders underneath my touch.

"You don't...you don't have to," he says. "I want you any way you'll let me have you. Even without the games."

"I'll call you whatever I like," I shoot back stubbornly, biting at his lip. "It's my game too. My fun too, whether I want you as Oliver or as my professor."

And again he shudders, but this time it's not only with lust. The wonder is back in his eyes, the awe. "How are you real?" he says, biting at my neck. "How can you possibly be real?"

Suddenly, I'm being carried, and I think it's inside, I think it's to his bed, but we end up tumbling over right in the lush grass below a cottage window, blown summer flowers bobbing all around us. His strong arms and hands protect me as we collapse onto the lawn, and above me is only the shape of a beautiful man outlined by stars.

"I want you," he manages in between searing kisses. "Now."

"Yes," I say eagerly, tugging at his clothes. "You won't hear any *red*s from me."

And it's the first time I hear a laugh from him that's real and open, not bleak at all.

"And please tell me you have a condom," I say, biting at his earlobe. "I can't wait a moment longer."

"You won't," he vows, pulling up. "You're mine now."

There are no houses around, and even if there were, we'd be completely surrounded by flowers and shrubs, but it's still insanely exhilarating to be like this, tumbled and tousled onto the lawn with my skirt bunched up around my thighs and Oliver on his knees between my legs, rolling on a condom. The feeling of being exposed, of being *filthy*, is enough to have me ready before Oliver even touches me.

"Oh, good girl," he murmurs when he tests my pussy to see if I'm wet and finds out exactly how wet I am. "Such a good girl."

I squirm under his touch. "Oliver..."

"I know, girl. Hold still." With a thick, urgent stretch, he fills me, and together we fuck under the stars until I cry out and he joins me in long, jerking pulses, and we roll giggling and grass-stained off the lawn and into the house.

CHAPTER TEN

OLIVER

I'm insatiable again, but I don't care. Maybe I'm making up for lost time, or maybe it's the heady pleasure of finding a woman who loves the way I am in bed.

Or maybe it's her.

Maybe it's this enthusiastic and boldly vulnerable girl who disarms me at every turn. This girl who warms my chest just with her smiles and with the way she holds her pen and her fucking adorable watch, who approaches dusty books with a zeal usually reserved for sex and religion. She gets under my skin, and I hate it and I love it all at once. And for a man who makes his living from words—studying them, analyzing them, writing them—I can't find the right words now to explain all this to her. That I want her, that she's mine, and that if she wanted, she could pluck out what's left of my heart and eat it, and I'd let her.

So I settle for telling her with my body. With my face between her legs, with my lips running along her thighs and stomach, with my mouth on her sweet tits. She begs to be spanked again, and this time I do it with her on all fours and my cock in her mouth, arranging her so that I can easily swat her ass from the side as she pleasures me.

Then we fuck again.

And again.

The early hours of the morning find us showered and sated, with her in my arms as I toy idly with her hair. I don't pretend it's only the oxytocin this time, and she doesn't ask, but I ask myself anyway.

What are you doing with her, Oliver?

What exactly are you doing?

And the answer is that I don't know, and it bothers me.

"Why are you ashamed of what you like?" Zandy asks softly, dreamily, like someone on the cusp of sleep.

I tense around her, the question taking me by surprise. Once again I'm struck by how *easy* this is for her, by how she can just ask and talk about these things like they're not...like they're not taboo. Like they're not twisted.

She senses my reticence and turns toward me, tilting her head up so she can see my face. "Oliver?"

I open my mouth and close it, the words just as elusive as they were earlier tonight.

"Was it Rosie?" Zandy asks, and she's so fearless, so brave, and it suddenly seems important to tell her so.

"You have so much courage," I murmur, stroking her cheek. "In your shoes, I'd never be able to ask about a lover's former flame."

Zandy blinks up at me in a very endearing manner. "I'm very plucky."

"I was going to say pugnacious. Or perhaps pesky."

She laughs, as always, at my surliness, and I melt a little.

I want to be brave and happy like her; I want to—I don't know—reward her, I suppose. Not like a professor rewards a student but how a lover rewards his lover. Vulnerability for vulnerability. Strength for strength.

Honesty for honesty.

"We met at the university I work for," I say finally. "We met, and it seemed like, oh, I don't know, all those stereotypes about falling in love. Like the world grew a thousand times bigger." I successfully keep most of the old bitterness from my voice, but there's enough that Zandy still notices, a little line appearing between her eyebrows. I reach over and smooth it with my thumb.

"Was she the first person you ever got kinky with?" Zandy asks, and again that word *kinky*, like it's just a word and not a rebuke. Not something I've tortured myself with in the years since Rosie left me.

"She was."

Zandy runs her hand in lazy circles over the muscles of my chest, playing slowly over the lean ridges of my abs. It feels impossibly nice. "Did she like it? The kinky stuff?"

"At first," I say, and the words leave me heavily. "At first. It was new to me—all of it was new. I was only just realizing what I liked and what I needed, and I think it became too real in the end."

"Because you were her professor?"

"I wasn't her professor," I reply. "She was mine."

Zandy's fingers still on my skin, and I can tell I've surprised her. "She was?"

"We met as I was studying for my PhD. I'd like to say that

we restrained ourselves until such a time when a liaison was ethical, but that would be a lie."

"You wouldn't be the first couple to start that way," Zandy says, and it warms me a little bit to see this young thing trying to comfort me. "So were the roles reversed? Did she do the spanking?"

There's a hint of a tease in her voice, and I give her a mock-stern tweak to the chin. "I always do the spanking, Miss Lynch. And I think the reversal of our power dynamic in the classroom is what excited her at first. For her, it was novel. To me, it became necessary."

I find that I miss Zandy's hand moving over my skin, and I wish she'd keep stroking me as I talked. Even with her, the first person I've felt a desire to open up to in years, it's not an easy story to tell. "We had about a year together. And then she got pregnant."

Zandy stiffens in my arms. "You have a child?"

"Miss Lynch, listen when your professor is talking." It's the closest I've come to a joke around her, and the answering smile on her face is worth everything. I resolve to do and say whatever I have to in order to make her smile more often.

"I was dazed when she told first told me she was pregnant," I continue. "Too dazed to be either elated or terrified, I think, but I offered her everything I could. I offered all of my support. I offered to quit my PhD program or transfer to another university so that I could marry her. I was ready to give up any part of my life I had to in order to make it work."

"And what did she say?"

"That she wanted a paternity test," I say, and in my mind,

I can still see us arguing in that dimly lit flat, the rain pouring outside and the blank expression on Rosie's face.

"What?" Zandy asks.

"The baby wasn't mine," I explain.

"But then—*oh*." I can see as she puts it together. The timelines, the evidence of infidelity. "Oh."

"She didn't want it to be mine. She was very blunt about that. She was very blunt about...well, lots of things. She'd been unhappy for some time, hence the cheating."

"That bitch," Zandy mutters, and her ferocious loyalty makes something in my chest impossibly light but tight too, like a balloon.

"Well, it was partially my fault. We'd grown into our bedroom games together, you see, and sometimes when something happens organically, you forget to communicate about it. And that's what happened with Rosie. I was happy, so I thought she was happy."

"Would she have been happy without the kink, you think?"

A fair question and one I've asked myself every day since that fight. All the names she called me, all the reasons she didn't want to raise a child with me, they've rattled around my mind for so long that they've become part of me, like a tree growing around a fence.

Degenerate.

Deviant.

Pervert.

"It's hard to say. I offered that too, to give up the professor games, but she refused... I think she resented me too much by then. The last time she spoke to me was an email informing me the test had proved the baby was his."

"Did you want the baby to be yours?"

I sigh. "I don't know. Yes...and no. I think the idea of a child with a woman you love always seems thrilling, but in retrospect, she didn't love me and I'm not even sure I loved her. Not in a lasting way, at least."

She moves her head, nodding against my shoulder in understanding, her hair sliding all silky and sweet smelling over my skin.

Either the memory's teeth have blunted over the years or something about Zandy eases the ache, but I find that I feel okay about the past. About Rosie. It's hard to feel upset about anything that led to this moment, with Zandy's soft curves tucked against my side and her hands on my body like it belongs to her.

"What happened after you broke up? Did you do the kink with anyone else?"

I think back to the intervening years between Rosie and now. I was a mess, both personally and professionally, and I owe a lot to the friends who saw me through, like Zandy's father, who helped me in every way he could. "I saw a few people, nothing serious. The kind of hookups you arrange online, that kind of thing. It got old after a while because it wasn't the same without someone I also liked and respected on an intellectual level."

She grins up at me. "Does this mean you like me, Professor Graeme?"

I give her a playful scowl and tug on her hair. "Don't push your luck, Miss Lynch."

She nestles back into me with a little yawn. "That explains why you're such a stickler about the condoms," she says. "The baby thing."

"Precisely so."

"Do you want babies someday? Or has that all been ruined?"

"So blunt, Miss Lynch."

But she's not asking in a fishing way—rather like she genuinely wants to know, and I think about it. About how Rosie was recently promoted to department head at my university and how there was no avoiding her then. No avoiding the very pregnant belly with her third child inside and her giant wedding ring. I took this sabbatical right after.

Deviant.

Degenerate.

"No," I finally answer. "I think that door has shut for me."

"That's sad," Zandy says sleepily.

I suppose it is sad, but I can't imagine going through all that again. The hope and the joy, and then the shame and the disgust...the heartbreak. Better just to avoid it entirely.

After a few minutes, I say, "I don't think kinky professors get to have babies and wives," and I'm rather proud of myself for saying the word *kinky* out loud...until I realize the girl next to me is fast asleep and snoring against my chest.

CHAPTER ELEVEN

ZANDY

When I wake up the next morning, Oliver is across the pillow from me, his beautiful river-colored eyes all soft and gentle on my face.

"Good morning, Miss Lynch," he says with a smile that's small but open and real, and I feel my heart dipping low inside me, like it's weighed down with happiness and is going to sink right through the mattress.

"Good morning," I answer in a sleep-croak, and then I make a face. My breath must be awful, not to mention the makeup I surely have smeared around my face. Of course he looks gorgeous right now, with that perfect, haughty face and his even more perfect hair. I try to roll away, and he catches me. "No," I moan, ducking my head into my pillow to try to hide my morning self. "I need to clean up."

"And you may, but I have to know, Zandy, were you planning on leaving last night?"

His voice is husky from sleep too, but it's also more vulnerable than I've ever heard him. Gentler. As if he's already bracing himself for the answer.

"Yes," I say honestly, because I do like to be honest. "But not anymore."

His brows furrow the slightest bit, and it's just so unfairly handsome on him that I can't stand it. I kiss him with my terrible morning mouth and get out of bed.

"So you're staying?" he asks, and the vulnerability is louder than ever, filling in the spaces between the words and lighting something very young and sad-looking in his face.

"Yes, Oliver. I'm staying."

Relief illuminates his face, and I'm rewarded with another one of those massive smiles, so big there are lines around his mouth and eyes when he makes it.

"Even with the"—I see him struggle to say the word, but he manages it with only a little bit of a blush—"the kinky stuff?"

"Especially because of the kinky stuff," I assure him with a wink, and then I go find a shower and a toothbrush, a big smile on my own face.

♦ ♦ ♦ ♦

After I'm all cleaned up and ready to work, I find myself strangely slow to go down to the office. Which Oliver will I find there? It seemed like we connected last night and this morning, but I thought that the first time we made love here at the cottage, and I was wrong. I don't think I can bear it if I open the door to find another cold Oliver again. Not after what we've shared together.

So it's with a deep breath and a lot of bravery—and a pat on Beatrix's head for good luck—that I open the door to Oliver's study and walk inside.

He's already behind the desk and bent over his work, all tousled hair and long fingers and wide shoulders. That old-fashioned ink pen winks in the sunlight as it moves in deft motions across the page. He finishes penning something in his notebook, ends it with an efficient little flourish, and then deigns to notice my presence. When he looks up, his mouth is in that sharp frown I normally find so irresistible, although it terrifies me right now.

"Miss Lynch," he says brusquely, and my heart plummets to my feet. Is that what this is going to be? Is today going to be a repeat of yesterday?

Am I being rejected again?

But then Oliver leans back in his chair and studies me in a way that I recognize, with his pulse jumping in his throat and his eyes gleaming with hunger.

"Come here. I need a word."

I don't have to pretend to be shy or uncertain as I walk to the desk. My chest is being hammered at with a heartbeat that's out of control, pumping every kind of hormone every which way through my body, and my mind is racing through every possibility. Is this a game? Or is this real? Did he come down to the office and find something I'd done wrong? Did he come down here and suddenly realize he wanted me to leave after all?

When I get to his desk, he impatiently gestures for me to come around the other side, and so I do with some worry, biting my lip.

"We need to talk about your work," he says, pointing to a paper on the desk.

I'm already puzzled because this isn't my work. My work is all databases and bookshelves, and this is just a paper with a single line written across it in ink pen. When I get closer, however, I see what's written on the paper, and then I'm biting my lip for an entirely different reason.

Red means stop.

I look up at him, and while he's still frowning, there's a palpable thrum of excited lust around him.

This is a game, I realize. And he wants to make sure it's okay with me if we play. He wants to check, and I love how careful he is for a man who seems so aloof.

How can he think he's twisted inside when he's so clearly concerned about my safety and emotional comfort? And has been even since our first night together in the rain?

He's a good man, I think, *and he doesn't even know it.* This Rosie hurt him too much for him to see that his kinks don't make him some kind of depraved freak. They might make him dirty, yes, unique maybe—but dirty and unique in a way that fit me perfectly, and I'm going to prove it to him.

I'm going to show him how much the filthy whorls and loops of his personality fascinate me. How well they feed me and please my inner teacher's pet.

"I don't see the problem with my assignment, Professor," I say, giving him my best innocent face. "I thought I followed all the instructions you gave me."

He gives me a dazzling smile and reaches out to squeeze my hand once before settling back into his flinty look from earlier.

"You didn't," he says shortly. "And I'm afraid there's no time for you to rework the assignment."

"Please," I say, putting my hands in front of me and twisting them. I'm a little surprised at how easily it comes to me, my role, but it's because I do really want to please him and it's so easy to imagine how unhappily desperate I'd feel in these circumstances. "Please, I'll do anything. Just don't give me a bad grade."

He studies me, propping his head against his fingers and letting his eyes roam over my body with predatory leisure. "Anything?" he murmurs. "Do you need the grade so badly?"

"I do. Please, you know I do." I cast around for what I might really say if I were in some kind of academic trouble, letting the sharp judgment in his gaze affect me. I feel ashamed, as if I really have messed up an assignment, and I also feel so fucking turned on I can't think straight. "I'll do an extra assignment. Two extra assignments!" I add when he starts to shake his head.

"That won't work, unfortunately," he says. "Unless..."

I don't even have to pretend to light up, that's how real this all feels. "Yes? I'll do it. I promise I will."

"Fine," he sighs, "but it's highly unusual. I daresay you won't be making the same mistakes with your paper after this."

"Yes, sir."

His pulse jumps above the collar of his button-down. He likes that.

"Are you wearing knickers beneath that dress, Miss Lynch?"

"Professor?"

"Take them off. You won't need them for this."

"B-But, sir—" I pretend to protest, even though inside I'm already squirming with delight. Already thinking of his palm on my backside and his long, thick cock pumping inside me.

He cuts me a look that brooks no argument. "This is *your* grade. If you want to fix it, this is how."

I give my best impression of a timid pout, although I think he can see the grin threatening to break through as I shimmy out of my panties. He holds out an imperious hand, taking them expressionlessly and putting them in a desk drawer.

"My bra too?"

"Bra too."

I take off my bra from under my dress, a little clumsily, wondering if I should just peel the whole dress off but deciding I should follow his instructions literally for now. It does feel quite lewd after I hand him the bra, standing there in a thin dress with nothing underneath. The soft jersey against my sensitive nipples only pulls them tighter and tighter, and my breasts feel obscene like this, heavy and loose and hard-tipped. Oliver seems to agree, his eyes darkening as he takes in my curves under my dress.

"You have a filthy little body, Miss Lynch. It's fucking profane. It makes me think shameful thoughts, and do you know what happens to a man when he thinks thoughts like I'm thinking?"

I shake my head, even though my eyes drop down to his lap.

"That's right," he says. "My cock gets hard and it needs to come."

I lick my lips instinctively at the thought, and he growls.

"Up on the desk."

I'd expected to go over his lap, so my hesitation is real. "Sir?"

"You heard me, Amanda." The use of my full name isn't lost on me—he means business now, and I'd better listen.

And I wouldn't have it any other way...although the punishment for not listening might be kind of fun too.

I sit on the edge of the desk facing him, keeping my skirt primly around my knees, which of course he doesn't allow for long. He grabs at the hem and pushes it up to my waist, separating my knees with an impatient hand. The kiss of coolish morning air against my wet and swollen cunt is nearly unbearable—almost as unbearable as his wicked gaze taking in my most feminine place.

He wastes no time in inspecting my pussy, rubbing me with his long fingers and then spreading me open to see if I glisten for him yet. I do. I can hear it as he moves his fingers over me, and I take a strange kind of pride in showing off how wet I get for him, how needy and slutty he makes me. I don't want him to doubt ever that his needs are also my needs—that they get me off as surely as they do him.

"You are so fucking filthy," he swears, and I can see how fast his chest heaves under his button-down. "You like this, don't you? You wanted it."

"Yes," I breathe, my head lolling to the side as one finger probes inside. "I wanted it."

"I knew it. I've seen the way you watch me in class, Miss Lynch. It's improper. It's very wrong."

"I can't help it," I whimper, lost to our game and to the skilled massage of his finger inside my pussy.

"I bet you even failed your assignment on purpose, just to provoke me into punishing you."

"I had to," I gasp. The heel of his palm is rolling against my clit now, and my legs are spread as wide as they'll go as I shamelessly fuck his entire hand. "I didn't know how else to get you to notice me."

"You think I didn't notice you? Those eyes, so innocent, with that mouth that just begs for a cock? You think I didn't notice those wanton tits? How they spill over your bra when you bend over? How they jiggle when you move?" He breaks off on his own groan now, and I can see the painful-looking outline of his dick in his trousers, pressing so hard against the fabric that the shape of the flared crown is visible.

"I think you need to be taught a lesson, filthy girl," he growls. "I think you need to fix the mess you've made."

"Anything," I say, bucking wildly against his hand. I'm so close, so very close. "Anything you want."

He removes his hand so suddenly that I curl around its absence, whining at the loss. He ignores me, unfastening his belt and trousers and pulling out his penis. It's dark and thick, so hard that the skin at the top shines and I can make out every ridge of muscle and vein under the thin, velvety skin of it.

"Suck," he orders, and I comply eagerly, scrambling to my knees between his legs and taking the delicious organ into my mouth.

His answering moan is worth every discomfort I feel as he gently gags the back of my throat, as he winds his hands through my hair and guides me faster and deeper over him. I'm grateful for the guidance, as I'm still so new to this, and I let Oliver's tensing thighs and hitched breaths teach me where he likes my tongue, how deep he likes to linger.

"I should keep you as my pet," he mutters viciously to the top of my head. "Keep you under my desk sucking me all day. Keep you tied up and bent over my desk so I can fuck that pretty cunt whenever I get bored. What do you think?"

I make an assenting noise around his shaft, and he grunts his approval.

"Enough." He pulls me off his cock with a faint popping sound and then rolls on a condom he grabs from a drawer. He spreads his legs, using his thumb to press his erection away from his belly. The message is clear.

"Come fix your grade, Miss Lynch," he says huskily, and I crawl up into his lap as quickly as humanly possible, aching for that thick part of him to fill me up and ease the ache that's been there ever since we fell asleep last night.

"I've never..." I trail off as I pause over him, catching his gaze. I'm suddenly apprehensive about this, about being on top. Everything else we've done, he's taken total control of, he's guided me and taught me, but if we do it like this...my inexperience will be on display. All of my clumsy attempts will be right there for him to see.

"I like that you've never," he says in a low voice. "But you're a smart girl, aren't you? You'll figure it out."

Determination settles through me. I want to show him what a smart and good girl I am, even if I look foolish doing it. I lower myself until I feel the wide latex kiss of his tip at my opening, having to squirm and circle to get him worked inside.

"You feel bigger like this," I say as he stretches me. "Fuck."

"Language, Amanda," he chides. Other than holding himself up straight at the base, he makes no move to help me as I pant and shiver my way down his cock, impaling myself inch by thick inch, until I'm fully seated against him, so filled up with him that I can barely breathe.

My head drops to his shoulder, and he lets me sit there for a moment, quivering and misted with sweat. "Oh God," I mumble into his neck. "Oh my God."

His hands run appreciatively over the round swell of my bottom, up to my hips, and back down to my ass again. "Let's see you fix that grade, girl," he murmurs into my ear. "Get to work."

With my arms wrapped around his neck and my face still in his shoulder, I start to move, moaning as I do. I'm stretched so wide, crammed full of him, and every movement I make sends agonies of sensation all over me. Good agonies, bad agonies, I don't even know which anymore—just that this colossal erection is going to split me open and also that I'm about to come from the pressure of it alone.

It only takes the tiniest of movements—a rocking forward so that my weight grinds the bead of my clit against him—and then I shudder out a deep, soul-shaking climax, clinging to him and crying my pleasure into his neck. He holds completely still underneath me, allowing me to quiver my way through and use his hard body how I need, and then he cups my bottom again with his hands as I collapse against his chest, utterly exhausted.

"That was very nice," he says crisply, as if I've just finished a violin solo and not wrung out a delicious orgasm on his perfect cock. "But I'm afraid it's not enough to fix your grade."

"Do you need to come, Professor?" I ask, sitting up and letting my hands fall to his chest. Even through the fabric of his button-down, I can feel the tattoo of his heart beating against my palm.

"Yes," he says, and he can use that precisely clipped voice all he wants, because his need is stamped all over his face. It burns inside his eyes and carves itself around the sharp lines of his sculpted mouth. "I need to come now."

It's both easier and harder to move along him—easier because of how wet and slippery I am and harder because the orgasm has made me exquisitely sensitive—and Oliver is riveted by my face as I begin to rock against him. His fingertips trace the fleeting furrows in my brow, the little pouts of pleasure and quick smiles I make. There's feeling everywhere, everywhere, chasing all over my skin; my nipples are so taut they ache, and my thighs are warm with his hips between them, and even the soles of my feet are tickled by the gentle breeze coming through the open window. I'm going to come again, and I don't think I'll live through it when I do.

Luckily, Oliver is close, and with something between a growl and a roar, he surges off his chair with me in his arms and lays me out across his desk. Papers go everywhere, the inkwell smashes over and spatters us with dark ink, and he's so mindless with his lust that he doesn't care. I watch a drop of ink trace down his neck like onyx-colored blood as he fucks me with a clenched jaw and powerful hips, and that line of ink is all that anchors me to reality as I come for an explosive, final time, too tired and wrung out to do anything other than whimper my way through it, my hands curling weakly around his straining biceps.

"You make me come so good," he grunts, his eyes closing as his body goes rigid over mine. "Fuck...Zandy...oh my fucking God."

He fills the condom with a series of hard, jerking throbs, slumping over my body as he drains inside me. Our hearts pound together, ink and sweat smears between us, and I'm pretty sure everyone from Bakewell to Berlin heard me screaming and grunting, but I don't even care. I don't ever want to move. I don't ever want to get clean. I don't ever want Oliver's body anywhere but right here, inside mine and pressed against mine and dripping ink everywhere.

And I look into his eyes where they peer down at me in their dappled blue-brown-green, and I can almost imagine he feels the same way.

I can almost imagine that we're falling in love.

CHAPTER TWELVE

OLIVER

Ten Days Later...

"I still don't understand what it is about slippers that you associate with advanced age."

Zandy and I are down by the river behind the house, and I'm meant to still be working, but I've given up. I thought by moving us out of the office that I wouldn't be tempted to fuck her, but as it turns out, I want to fuck her everywhere, and I very nearly have.

In the past two weeks, I've fucked her uncountable times over my desk, on my study floor, in my bed, in my shower, and on my kitchen table. I've spanked her until she's been a wet, whimpering mess. I've made her write essays naked at her desk. I've had her service me with her mouth under my desk while I finished taking notes on a Victorian pamphlet about marriage proposals. We've spent nearly every hour together, working and talking and fucking and sometimes just with her curled in my lap kissing me until we're both breathless and beyond speech. Every meal, every shower, every mug of passable tea in the last two weeks has happened with her by my side.

And I haven't hated it.

I haven't hated it at all.

Somehow, someway, Zandy has made my life sweeter, and a callous, terrible part of me wants to dismiss it as a natural result of all the fucking, but the rest of me knows better. This thing I have with Zandy is remarkably different than whatever I had with Rosie—better and more honest and more real— but there's enough of the same for me to recognize what's happening.

I care for Zandy.

Although as I watch her pick her way around the riverbank, looking for stones and ignoring my comment about slippers, I know I can do better than *I care for her*.

I'm falling in love with her.

And it makes me angry and terrified and excited, and I'm not sure what to do about it. I'm not sure I *should* do anything about it. After all, she's young and vibrant and has an entire life waiting for her at the end of the summer. The last thing she wants is some surly bastard making claims to her life.

It stings though, thinking that these days of splashing in the river and wandering up to town after a long day of work are numbered. Listening to the quiet rustle of her writing on the other side of the room, looking forward to tangling my limbs around hers at night.

But it would be ridiculous to want more than the summer. In fact, I can't believe I'm even thinking about it. Of course she needs to leave—her life is in the States and my life is here, and my life doesn't include another person, no matter how sexy or warm or open she is. Never mind how much she looks at me like I matter, like my needs matter, like I'm not a deviant but someone she adores.

She won't adore you for long. Rosie couldn't.

With that depressing reminder, I look up to see Zandy climbing the riverbank toward me, green blades of wet grass sticking to her feet. She flops onto the blanket next to my pile of books with a sigh.

"I won't apologize for the slippers," she says, finally addressing my comment from earlier. "Only old people wear them."

"Objectively not true, as I wear them."

She wrinkles her nose at me. "But why?"

"The floors get cold," I say defensively. "I have cold floors."

"And then there's the old man pen."

"It has character."

"And the old landscape paintings."

I bristle a little. "Those are tasteful."

Those soft lips are creased in a teasing smile, and I realize she's poking fun at me. I crawl over her body and pin her to the blanket.

"I believe," I whisper against her lips, "that you're being very impertinent at the moment, Miss Lynch."

She wriggles happily underneath me, her dark-blue eyes glowing with her smug little smile. "And I suppose impertinent girls have to be punished, Professor?"

"How right you are," I growl before sealing my mouth over hers in a fierce kiss, licking against her tongue until she moans up into me. But I decide I can't wait, and I start shoving up the skirt of her dress right then and there.

"Do you have a condom?" she asks breathlessly, her hands already at work to shimmy out of her panties.

I've been obsessive about having one—or three—with me at all times, but I'd genuinely thought I'd be able to control myself this afternoon. "Fuck, darling," I say, giving her a quick kiss. "I'll run in and get one."

"Hurry." She pouts as I get off the blanket, and it's a true test of my strength to leave her like this, with her gleaming hair in a dark halo around her head and her bare pussy already wet and waiting for me.

"I will," I vow, and I stride quickly inside. When I get to my bed table, I realize we've already gone through Zandy's condoms and the new package she bought at the store last week. With a sigh, I dig out the old box at the back of my drawer—the one I've had for an embarrassingly long time—and grab a condom, briefly checking the expiry date as I do. With a sigh of relief that we're still, only just, inside the date, I am downstairs and behind the house as quickly as my legs will carry me. I fall over Zandy like a hungry wolf, eating up her giggles and sighs as if they'll feed me through the winter.

And before long, I'm sheathed and pushing between her legs, relishing the velvet, tight grip of her as I pierce her deep. Fuck, she feels so good. She always feels so good. She's always so soft and tight, always pure heaven to fuck into.

I angle my hips the way I know she likes, pumping into her with strokes that drag along her most sensitive spots, and she's a wild thing beneath me, being both a very good and a very bad girl at the same time, as only she can. I steal another aggressive kiss, wishing I could steal everything of hers and keep it forever—not just her beauty and her extravagant body but her laugh and her intellect and her fearlessness. All the things that make her so perfectly Zandy are the same things that flay me open and make me want to be a better Oliver, a man kind and smart and brave enough to deserve her.

"Oliver," she whispers against my lips, and I feel the telltale flutters in her belly and inner thighs and around my cock—she's going to come. I add my thumb to her clit as I brace myself on a forearm over her, but right as she goes over the edge, I feel something I can't recall feeling before. It feels like a pop, a tiny pop, and then all of a sudden there's a new feeling of warmth and wet.

"Shit," I gasp, pulling out as fast as I can.

"What?" the girl under me says dazedly, still coming down from her climax. "What is it?"

"I think the condom broke."

That's sufficient information to alarm her, and she props herself up on her arms as I peel off the condom and examine it. "But it's okay, right?" she asks worriedly. "Since you haven't come yet?"

"I think so," I say, still peering at the condom in the afternoon sun. It's definitely broken. "It's probably because it's old..."

And then I have a real chill when I remember that old box was the source of my condom in London. Did that condom break without me realizing it? I'm nearly lost to panic at the idea, until something very warm and wet closes over my bare cock, and I look down to see those devilishly soft lips closing around my shaft. Her tongue is everywhere, flickering and soft beyond imagination, and she takes me deep like I prefer, deep enough that her throat squeezes the head of my cock.

I groan.

And as she fucks me with her mouth, I forget all about old condoms and terrifying possibilities and lose myself to Zandy and the warming feeling of coming in the afternoon sun with the river rushing sweetly beside us.

◆ ◆ ◆ ◆

The next day, I propose a work break, and Zandy and I go to Haddon Hall for a lunch of sandwiches and a stroll through the medieval manor.

"Why library school?" I ask as we walk through room after room and she chatters at me about all the architectural details and historical oddities tied to them. "It's clear that you love history. And," I say, a little shyly because I'm strangely unused to giving compliments, "you're damned knowledgeable about it, and you're a fucking good researcher to boot."

She has to hide a beaming little smile at my praise, and it does something to my chest. A puffing thing. I have the power to do that—I have the power to make her happy. I want to make her beam all the time; though as soon as I realize that, I remember that I can only make her beam until the summer is through.

"I could never decide on just one thing that fascinated me," she says, stepping into the long gallery and then spinning in a slow circle to take it in. "Like this building. It's a medieval manor house with a Tudor-style gallery and Victorian monuments in the chapel. I like the idea of my mind being full of layers and chambers and niches and naves, each one filled with different things. As a historian, you have to pick, but as a librarian...you get to have it all."

Her speech is rather charming, even if I feel slightly specious in its reasoning, but it's *her* I am truly held captive by—the way her eyes glow as she speaks, the way her body animates with enthusiasm. "Fine," I concede. "But why school in Kansas? You could go anywhere you'd like—why not somewhere more prestigious?" If she wants libraries, she deserves the best libraries in the world. She deserves everything.

"I'll have you know that there are some very good library schools in Kansas," she sniffs. And then after a moment, she adds quietly, "And I didn't want to leave my dad."

"Why not?" I live less than fifty miles away from my parents, and I still only see them twice a year, and that's more than fine by me. "He's not unwell...or anything?"

She rolls her eyes. "He's perfectly fine, health wise. I just think family is important, don't you?"

I suppose the time it takes for me to reply is answer enough. She examines me for a moment. "Does this have anything to do with why you're so weird about money?" she asks.

"I'm not *weird* about money," I protest, but even as I protest, I lower my voice so no one around us can hear.

She makes a *you're proving my point* face, and I sigh.

"Okay, yes, my family has some money." Even that vague admission feels unclean. "And there's no trauma, no division, but the way they are about what they have is very old-fashioned to me. I try to avoid it and I think they try to avoid me."

And then I let out a breath. It didn't kill me to say it out loud, and it actually felt nice, a little bit, telling someone about how unpleasant my family can be.

"That wasn't so hard, was it?" she asks, taking my hand and pulling me to a cove of mullioned windows to admire the green expanse outside. "Maybe you just need the right family, you know? One that fits you."

And the strange thing is that I'm looking at her as she says that, as she gazes through the diamond patterns of glass out onto the verdant expanse of grass and hills, and I'm thinking of *her*. I'm thinking of her as my family.

It tempts me more than I can bear.

But I force myself to remember the ticking clock of summer. Force myself to remember Rosie's cruel words all those years ago.

Degenerate.

Deviant.

Even if we didn't have that date in August demarcating our time, how could I ever expect someone as full of promise and innocence to want to tie herself to a monstrous recluse like me? Zandy might think these kinds of games are fun for a summer, but how could she ever want someone like me for longer? Someone as contorted and sexually corrupt as me?

At the end of the day, Zandy will be the same as Rosie, and she'll be sick of me. It's better to prepare myself for that now and plan for a clean break, no matter how much it burns to think of it.

No matter how much it hurts.

CHAPTER THIRTEEN

ZANDY

It occurs to me the next day.

I'm at the kitchen table making a shopping list, and then I have to double check the date on my phone. I run upstairs and riffle through my things and see that I've only got a handful of travel-worn tampons to call my own, and my period is due to start any day now. I trot back downstairs and add tampons to the list, along with the various foodstuffs and household supplies Oliver needs. If I didn't shop for him, I think he'd probably survive on canned soup and tea. It's a little charming in a bachelor kind of way, if it isn't also a little stupefying.

The day proceeds as normal—I work, Oliver fucks me, I shop, Oliver fucks me again—and it's as I'm snuggling to sleep in Oliver's arms that I wonder how we'll navigate my period. I've never done this before, the whole lover thing, and I'm not sure what the protocol is. Do I give him a warning that it's coming, or do I just wait until it's arrived and apologize? Will he still be okay fooling around on my period?

And what if he still wants to have sex? Am I comfortable with that?

It's a lot to digest, and so I'm still thinking over it as I fall asleep, and again as I wake up to Oliver stroking my flanks in a way that lets me know he's thinking about spanking me.

We do a morning spanking and a morning fuck, and then it's time for the day to get on, except there's a little niggle of unease at the back of my mind.

No period yet.

I shower and go downstairs, and he gets in from his run and showers too, and we work together for most of the day, my sense of unease growing. But I have no idea how to vocalize it to him, no idea how to express my worries, because what if his first thought is of Rosie? What if he's so triggered by his bad pregnancy experience with her that he gets angry with me?

Or worse, what if he thinks I'm the clingy girl who's tried to trap him into something by getting pregnant?

Oh God. Just the thought itself is enough to make me nauseous...except, was I already nauseous? Am I truly nauseous now? No. I'm overreacting, I'm just queasy from nerves and worry, that's all. Nothing to do with *that*.

Except the next morning when I wake up in Oliver's arms, I am *definitely* nauseous. For real nauseous. I slide free of him and make my way to the bathroom, where I splash my face with cold water and force myself to get *un*-nauseous.

He said the condom broke that day by the river.

But that was just two days ago. I've done enough research to know that conception could have only happened two weeks or so ago, and that would have been in London, and I'd bought all of those condoms brand new. But...

We used one of his condoms in London.

Oh God.

No.

"No," I say out loud, just to make extra certain my brain processed the word. "No. This is not happening."

This can't be happening.

I go downstairs in only my thin cotton robe and make my way down the flagged path to the river. It's still very early morning, with only a faint-pink sun and river fog like a shroud over everything, and more than life itself, I want to go crawl back in bed with the handsome, snobby professor I've come to love.

Oh shit. *Do* I love him? Because this is a hell of a time to decide. But even with my lingering nausea and fear, I think I know the answer.

Yes.

Yes, of course, I love Professor Graeme. His dirty games and his sharp words and his brilliant intellect. His rare flashes of warmth and kindness, his hidden passion and fire just waiting for the right person to patiently uncover them...

I love him.

And I may be pregnant with his child, and somehow I just *know* he'd never forgive me if that were true, no matter how innocent of it I may be. No matter how accidental, no matter how not my fault, the one wound he bears is so deeply tied to a baby, and how can I, just a silly little student, ever hope to heal him of it?

First thing's first, I order myself. No sense in worrying about something that might not even be true. I'll get dressed and find a pharmacy and get a pregnancy test. And then I can decide what comes next and what it means for my professor and me.

♦ ♦ ♦ ♦

I'm to the pharmacy and back to the cottage before Oliver is finished with his run, and I have a plan. I'll go to the bathroom—the small water closet by the snug, the one we hardly ever use—and I'll use the tests. Yes, *tests* plural, because I couldn't decide on a brand, and despite having everything from the best nursing bras to the best infant formula, *Consumer Reports* doesn't have a buying guide for pregnancy tests. So I bought three different brands of pregnancy tests, just to be safe.

But when I lock myself inside the bathroom, I'm gripped by a slow, creeping hesitation. Like I'm being gradually, gradually frozen in ice, until I'm sitting on the floor across from the sink with my head between my legs just staring at the tile. The nausea from the early morning has faded, leaving only a tingling kind of displacement in its place, like my stomach and my heart have traded places.

Just go pee on that stick. Just do it.

But even standing up right now feels like a herculean feat—like if I stand up, I'm accepting whatever happens next, and I'm not sure I can do that.

I'm not sure I'm strong enough to do that.

But as romantic as it would be to spend the rest of the day on the floor in a state of languishing gloom, I'm not immune to the ticking clock of Oliver's run. And my ass is cold from the tile. And my own despair is getting a bit boring—it's not like me to despond over a problem. It's like me to tackle the problem head-on, with research and enthusiasm and a big Zandy Lynch grin, and dammit, that's what I'm going to do now.

So I get up and perform the oddly ignoble ritual of peeing on the different sticks and then lining them up according to size and waiting and watching.

It's strange to think that my entire future is concentrated in these little plastic rectangles full of urine and chemical dyes. Strange to think that whatever these rectangles reveal in the next minute or two is going to completely redirect the course of my life for better or for worse, and oh my God, they're finally starting to turn colors, they're finally starting to stripe over with weak washes of blue and—

I sit back down on the floor, except this time I don't stare at the tile, I stare at my hands, as if I expect them to be different. As if I expect my entire body to be different.

Nothing's different.

But everything is. Everything has to be.

Because I'm pregnant, and I'm pregnant with a baby I know Oliver won't want.

◆ ◆ ◆ ◆

I set a timer on my phone and give myself five minutes. Five minutes to freak out—to scream or to cry or whatever I need to do—and then when the timer beeps, I wipe away my tears, sweep the tests with their condemning plus signs into the trash, and go find my laptop to make a plan.

Oliver comes into the study with shower-damp hair and rolled-up sleeves that show off the strong lines of his forearms and wrists. He's scrubbing at the wet hair with his fingertips and frowning in that way that tells me he's already several layers deep into some new insight of his, but he stops when he sees me at my desk and he smiles.

God, that smile.

It's so wide, with lines bracketing those sculpted lips, and it changes his entire face from scornfully distant to sincere and boyish.

"Good morning, Miss Lynch," he says, and I slam my laptop shut so he won't see all the incriminating tabs I have open, and I smile back at him, hoping he won't see how forced it is.

"Good morning, Professor," I say, and then he bends in to kiss my neck. He didn't shave this morning, and his stubble leaves the most delicious burn wherever his soft lips touch me. It's the best kind of sting, and for a minute I let everything else fade away—the pregnancy, the panic, the plan—and just melt into the feeling of him. My professor. My Oliver.

He withdraws too soon, dropping a kiss on my head before he goes to his desk. "You've nearly finished with all the books, I see."

"I still have a lot of the newer ones to do," I say automatically, and then I stop myself because I don't know that I'll get to the newer books. I don't know that I'll be able to get to anything else at all, because I don't know what's going to happen after I tell Oliver I'm pregnant.

Unless you don't tell him...

The idea is beyond tempting. It snakes around my thoughts and my heart until I feel tied up with it.

"Whenever you have time," Oliver says, not noticing my inner struggle. "I'm already astounded at what you've accomplished in just a couple short weeks."

Despite everything, I allow my gaze to follow his around the study, and I don't bother to tamp down the bubble of pride I feel at the progress I've made. Instead of an unsteady maze made of piles of books and paper, I've got the study organized with new shelves and cabinets of glass-topped drawers for the rarer works. Aside from the books stacked under my desk still awaiting cataloguing, the floor in the study is now completely clear—save for the cat bed I bought on a whim for Beatrix—and a person can actually walk around the room without tripping onto centuries-old manuscripts now.

I *have* done a good job here, and I'll be able to take that with me no matter what. I look over to the unbearably handsome man already bent over his work, and I can't help but think that's possibly all I'll get to take with me: the memory of well-shelved books and nothing else.

The thought punches through my chest with grief, and I have to turn away, lest I risk Oliver seeing all these wild emotions move across my face. No, it's best I approach him as controlled and composed as possible. I need to be cold like him.

By the end of the afternoon, I've done all the surreptitious research I can. I've made a spreadsheet of options, along with their qualitative pros and their quantitative cons. I've found a flight home from Birmingham, and I've begun preparing a small speech to Oliver, with a few salient bullet points.

Namely, that this is not my fault—if it's anyone's fault, it's *his*, for using old-ass condoms—and also, second bullet point, I'm keeping the baby. I've made a *spreadsheet* and I've made a decision, and a spreadsheet decision is a permanent one.

Maybe it's insane—maybe I'm insane—but when I sat there looking at all the different paths I could take, my hand kept drifting to my belly and my mind kept drifting to this fantasy of a baby with Oliver's multicolored eyes.

Maybe...maybe he won't be angry? Maybe he won't be terrified? Maybe he's healed enough from what happened with Rosie that he can imagine a little squishy baby with his eyes and my dimples and all will be well?

But what if he doesn't? What if he can't?

What if I tell him and confess to loving him, and he rejects both me and the baby in one fell swoop? What then?

Then you take the flight out of Birmingham and get started on your baby to-do list.

I curl over my desk, bracing my head against my hands, and try not to cry. I don't want to be rejected. I don't want to lose Oliver. And yet, even without the baby, I don't know that he'd want me. He hasn't mentioned anything about an *us*, about this being anything more than a convenient, kinky fling to while away the summer.

I want more than anything to be reasonable, to be logical, but maybe it's the pregnancy hormones or maybe it's the fact that Oliver stirs me up beyond reckoning, but suddenly, the tears are right there, ready to fall. Am I so unlovable? So unlikable? That even something longer than a summer with me is a detestable thought?

"Zandy." A low voice comes from behind me, and I freeze as Oliver's warm hands slide over my shoulders. "Are you okay?"

In my distress, I completely forgot that he could see and

hear me. I hoped he was too absorbed in his work to notice my breakdown, but it appears I was wrong.

Like I've been wrong about so much else.

"I'm fine," I say, pressing the heels of my palms against my eyes and swallowing back my emotions. I move my hands and look up at him, giving him my brightest smile. "Just tired."

He frowns. "I've been working you too hard."

"Not at all," I say, grateful that no tears have actually spilled and now only wishing the tremble in my chin would settle. "Really, I'm fine. I probably just need a nap."

And before I can protest—or indeed, even process what's happening—Oliver's scooping me up in his arms and carrying me up the stairs.

"Oliver!" I say, tugging pointlessly at the shirt fabric near his neck and kicking my legs weakly. "Put me down!"

"You're having a nap," he says firmly, carrying me into his bedroom and laying me on the bed. He stands over me, as if torn. Then he climbs onto the bed as well, not to cradle me in his arms but going lower, lower, until his wide shoulders are tucked between my legs.

"This—this isn't a nap," I say breathlessly as he pushes my skirt up to my waist and tugs my panties to the side.

"I'm tucking you in," he says, a single eyebrow arching in mischief. "Making sure you can fall asleep easily."

And I could cry as his mouth descends warm and wet on my intimate flesh, not because I was near to tears before but because I love him so much, because he's made me fall in love with him, because I can hardly stand these rare glimpses of his open, happy soul and I'm terrified I'll have to leave them behind with everything else. I'm terrified of sending him back into his emotionless, cruel shell once I tell him the truth. My mischievous, smiling professor will be gone, and all that will be left is a bitter husk in his place.

You can't know that, I assure myself, although the assurance feels hollow. There's every chance I'll tell Oliver and things will go well. There's every chance this has a happy ending.

But I can't stop the tide of doubt that seeps in along with the tide of pleasure, and as his mouth gently works me toward climax, I find myself clinging on to every single sensation, every single slice of memory. His soft hair under my fingers and his hot mouth and teasing hands pressing and massaging and stroking at all of my most sensitive places, and then finally—sweetest of all—the tender expression on his face as I come undone, pleasure spiraling out from my belly in whorls of ecstasy. I arch and writhe under him, my toes digging at the blankets, my head rolling back, and when I slowly circle back to earth, I see him standing up and getting ready to pull the blankets over me—as if he really means to tuck me in.

"What about you?" I ask, reaching for him.

He pauses, obviously torn. "I don't need—shit, Zandy. Holy shit..."

My hands have found him under his trousers, and I'm giving him a teasing squeeze. He's as hard as a spike.

"I'll just take a minute," I promise, and he growls, already mounting the bed and unfastening his pants.

"The hell you will," he says darkly, and then my lips are being parted by the plump, swollen head of his cock as he feeds it into my mouth.

"Fuck," he hisses as I instinctively suck around him. "Yes, girl, just like that, just like that." And after I've sucked him to his satisfaction, he pulls himself from my mouth and straddles my stomach, yanking down my dress and my bra to expose my tits. I love seeing him like this, feral and quaking with unfiltered lust, and there's something so primal about seeing a man normally as refined as Oliver do something as crude as mark me with his come. But that's what he does, his one hand braced on the headboard above me, and his other hand fucking his cock as if he'll die if he doesn't empty himself immediately. I watch the dusky head disappear and reappear in the ferocious circle of his grip, and then I moan in fascinated lust as his orgasm leaves him in thick, white ropes all over my bare tits.

It's so fucking erotic that I've nearly forgotten about everything that's come before, and I beg him to rub me again, to fix the new empty ache he's made inside me, and by the time we come again and clean up, we're both ready for a nap.

Tomorrow, I think drowsily as I fall asleep. *I'll tell him tomorrow.*

CHAPTER FOURTEEN

OLIVER

Zandy's been acting strange.

I noticed it yesterday before I whisked her up to my bed, and I'm seeing it again today as we start our work for the morning. And I think I know what it's about, which means I'm currently sitting at my desk ruminating not over a photographic illustration of the courtship process, as I should be doing, but over what I should do next.

I mean, it's obvious what I should do next. I should talk to her. But I'm a gelded coward, because even the mere thought of saying what I need to say out loud has me retreating.

A small sigh sifts over to me from Zandy's desk, and I look up to see her running the top of a pen along her mouth, along the seam of those sinful lips. She's got one hand spread low on her belly, and her eyes are distant. She's beautiful. Beautiful and smart, and she's pried open locks inside me that I thought were sealed shut for eternity.

What am I doing with her? Why can't I be as brave and reckless as she can, and why can't I just admit how I feel? Admit that I want her and love her and need her for longer than the summer?

Because that's what she needs, isn't it? That's what this new distance of hers is about? She's finally realized that I've given her nothing more substantial than my cock and the palm of my hand, and even though we promised nothing more between each other, it's catching up with her. She's adjusting her feelings and expectations, and....and I don't want her to. I don't want another morning like the one in London when I woke up alone. I don't want there to be any reason she thinks she has to leave me.

I want her to know how I feel.

"Zandy," I say softly. "Come here."

I've summoned her to my desk countless times since she's arrived at my home, but this is the first time *I* feel nervous as she approaches, the first time I have no idea what happens next. But despite that, my cock hardens as she walks toward me in her little tweed skirt and schoolgirl-ish blouse—exactly the kind of outfit that tempts me to distraction. I'm going to fuck her after we talk, I decide, to reward her for being so perfect.

She's ready to kneel or to bend over my desk, and her eyes flare with pleased surprise as I pull her down into my lap.

"Miss Lynch," I murmur, brushing some of that coffee-dark hair away from her face.

"Professor," she says, the word as always staining her cheeks with an adorable pink. I kiss those cheeks now, then her plush mouth, sliding my tongue against her lips until she opens for me and I can kiss her the way I want. Deep and devouring. Claiming and hungry.

"I love you," I say against her mouth, and the words leave me like my own breath, like water from a spring. As natural as anything, as easy as being alive. And at the sound of them in the gentle summer air of the office, I feel a surge of happiness so real that I can't believe I've waited so long to say them. I should have told her the minute I realized. I should have told her and then told her nothing else for the rest of my life.

Except while I'm smiling against her lips, I realize that Zandy's gone completely rigid in my arms, and when I pull back with a concerned gaze to look at her, I see nothing but pure panic in her face.

Dread sends my stomach plummeting to my feet, and suddenly a horrible thought wedges its way into my mind. What if she doesn't love me? What if she doesn't care for me at all? What if—oh God—all the sighs and the distant looks have been because she wants to be free of me? What if she wants to be free of my deviance? My perversions?

My *kink*, as she so innocently calls it?

It's Rosie all over again, except worse, a thousand times worse, because I didn't love Rosie like I love Zandy. Not even close, not even a little bit. If Zandy doesn't love me, I'm not sure I'll survive it.

But before I can complete my own terror spiral, I see that Zandy's sapphire eyes are brimming with tears, and I reach up to brush them away. She catches my hand with my fingertips on her cheek, nuzzling against my palm like a distressed kitten, and it breaks my heart to see her so upset. And it breaks my heart again to think that she might be upset because she's going to refuse me. Because I confessed to loving her and now she's trying to find the words to tell me that she doesn't love me back.

"Zandy," I say in a choked voice. "You don't have to—I mean, I shouldn't have—please don't—"

She presses her own fingers to my lips now, meeting my eyes with the shining blue of her own.

"I love you too, Oliver," she whispers, but she doesn't sound happy. She sounds anything *but* happy, and her words are like twin swords of joy and pain right to my heart.

Doesn't she feel it? How good and right we are? Doesn't she understand how huge this is for me, how fucking rare and perfect?

"Then why are you crying?" I ask, searching her face. "I don't understand."

She just shakes her head, crying even harder now, and she curls into the tiniest possible ball in my arms, until she's completely nestled into me and the scent of her hair fills my nose. Her legs are pulled up to her chest, which hikes her skirt past her ass, and even though my mind is mostly on soothing her, my body reacts to the rounded flesh now sitting bare on my leg.

And then her lips are on my neck, open and imploring, working their way up to my jaw and my earlobe, her tear-wet face slicking against mine, but I don't deny her. I can't deny her anything, I think, least of all the comfort I'm the most qualified to give.

I meet her mouth with an ardent kiss, tugging her against me so she has no choice but to straddle me, so her hard nipples press through her shirt and drag against my chest, so I can cup her backside in my hands and grind her against my cock for the friction we both crave. Her tongue, when I find it, is eager and needy, chasing mine with a desperation that's underscored by her hands flying everywhere—at my shirt buttons, at the bunched muscles of my arms, at the tensed lines of my neck.

"Oh, Oliver," she mumbles. "Please, please, please."

"Anything, darling," I say, the endearment slipping out of me faster than I can catch it back. But why would I want to catch it back? I love her. She deserves for me to be more than a tight-lipped miser about it.

She's already fumbling with my pants, her small, slender fingers on my cock, and before I can even register how good it feels to have her stroking the hot, thin skin, she's wedging me at her most private place and pushing herself down in wild, frantic thrusts.

It's messy and rough, her skirt bunched around her waist and tears still dripping from her face, but her eyes are completely open and raw on mine and something between us tightens closer than ever, like a knot being cinched shut. I should stop her. I should wipe her tears away. But how can I when the first edge of a smile pulls at her lips and she's chanting, "Yes, Oliver, oh God, yes"?

When she feels like pure fucking ecstasy on my cock, wet and slick and soft, like a tight heaven? It's never felt this good, *ever*. It's never been me clenching every muscle in my belly and ass and thighs so I don't blow too early. It's never been—

I've never been bare with her.

Holy shit.

Holy shit, I'm raw and naked inside her. I'm naked inside her, and it feels better than anything I've ever felt in my entire life. Ever. If I come like this, I don't even know how I'll survive, because I'm barely holding on as it is, and...

But I can't come like this. I *can't*. I've fucked that up before, and I refuse to fuck it up with Zandy. My bold little librarian with her entire life ahead of her; she's far too precious for me to make this mistake a second time.

My hands find her hips, and I try to still the frenzied roll of her body over mine. "Let me get a condom," I say to her. "This isn't safe."

She peers down at me, and for a moment, I treasure just how beautiful she is like this, even with tear tracks shining on her face. Her hair is like the silkiest, sweetest curtain around us, her cheeks are flushed and pink, and her mouth is a study in feminine glory.

"Oliver," she says. Just that. Just my name, and there's an undercurrent of pain in it, like it's the last time she'll ever say it like this, which is ridiculous, of course. If I have it my way, she can say it every day for the rest of her life.

I try to ease her off me. "Let me get prepared, Zandy. It will only take a second, and then you can ride me as long as you want."

She doesn't move yet, her lower lip trembling a little. "It feels so good," she says. "I didn't know it would feel different for me too, but it feels so good."

I give a taut, rough laugh. "Yes, it feels good. Too good, and if we don't fix it, I'm going to be coming inside you."

Her lower lip trembles even more. "What if it didn't matter?"

I stare up at her, my mind spinning even as my cock flexes in happiness at the thought. "But it does matter," I point out.

My chest tightens in irritated confusion, because how can she even joke about it not mattering? With her future? With my past?

She closes her eyes. "It doesn't have to. Not now."

"Because we've said I love you?" There's a spiked cynicism to my tone that I don't like, but I can't help it. "I've said those words before, Zandy. They have nothing to do with what will happen if I come inside you."

Her eyes flutter open, and suddenly I know I've said something wrong, something deeply wrong. "Right," she says faintly. "Of course." She tries to climb off my lap, but despite it being what I wanted, it feels wrong now, like if I let her un-join us, something else, something more crucial, will come un-joined as well. I hold her tight to me, catching her eye.

"Zandy?"

"No, it's fine," she says, still trying to move off me, and I have a flash where I realize I'm forcing her to stay on my lap. I let go of her as if I've been burned, horrified at the thought of forcing a woman, but I'm just as horrified at the look on her face when she gets to her feet in front of me. She looks like I've slapped her, and I don't know if it's because I let her go or because of what I said.

She pulls down her skirt, and I have the distinct impression that she's trying to make herself look more dignified, more adult, as if that matters when my cock is still naked and wet between us.

"Do you mean that? What you said about love having nothing to do with fucking bare?"

She's twisted my words, but as much as I work with words

for a living, I can't figure out how. It's in the tone, in her giant blue eyes so wounded and the way she wraps her arms around herself, as if to shield her body from me.

"I meant," I say slowly, "that just because I love you doesn't give me permission to be reckless. In fact, *because* I love you, I don't want to be reckless. Not with your future."

Something softens in her face, and her lip quivers again. "What if my future's already changed?" she asks.

"You don't understand what I mean, sweetheart. I mean—"

"I'm pregnant," she blurts out. "I just found out yesterday. I'm pregnant."

There's a kind of static buzzing in my ears, like the air itself has come to life to hiss the truth at me, but it doesn't matter because I find myself groping clumsily for both thoughts and words.

It doesn't make any sense is the first real thought that surfaces, coupled with, *but I was so careful.*

So careful to use protection every single time, so careful to avoid repeating the mistakes of the past. So careful not to ever put myself in that hideous situation again.

I hope it isn't yours.

Pervert.

My silence hasn't gone unnoticed by Zandy, and her face and voice are just on the edge of crumpling when she says, "It must have been in London. I'm not on birth control, and if your condom broke..."

Didn't I think it was all too wet that night when I went to take it off? But who could blame me for not thinking about it when I was still reeling with the fact that she'd *been a virgin*?

Yes, the condom was old, but it wasn't so old that I thought twice as I rolled it on, and holy fuck, what were the damn odds? That the night she lost her virginity was also the night she got pregnant?

And it's that more than anything that makes the blood drain from my face, that makes my body cool and grow rigid with self-loathing.

I'm no better than the pervert Rosie thought I was, impregnating some innocent like a fucking caveman, no matter how accidental it was. I pull my pants closed, fumbling for an apology, for anything to convey the sheer fucking horror I feel about what I've done to her, but I'm coming up with nothing, and it's only as I look up at her again that I realize the damage my lack of response has caused.

My silence has cost me something important, although I'm not yet sure what it is.

Because the trembling lip is gone. The tears have dried up. In their place is an expression of blazing determination— not unlike her face the night we met, but there's something heartbreakingly grim in her look now, like she's resigned herself to a future so cold that it's already making her numb.

I sit up, about to say something, anything, just to forestall whatever is about to come out of her mouth, but she speaks first.

"I've already found a flight home," she says clearly, "so I don't want you to worry about me lingering here when I'm unwanted."

Unwanted?

But her reasoning slips by me as I face the reality of what she just said.

She's leaving me.

Not only is she leaving me, but she's already made the plans, which means she's been thinking about leaving me for... bloody Nora, maybe since she found out. Maybe since the moment she realized she was pregnant.

The thought chills me down to my core.

Just like Rosie. She can't stand the idea of carrying my child.

"...a spreadsheet," Zandy is saying, still standing in front of me like she's delivering the bleakest presentation of all time. "And I'm keeping the pregnancy. I've thought about it within both rational and emotional parameters, and it's the decision I feel the happiest with. I know, obviously, you aren't happy and that you won't want anything to do with me or the child, and I promise I won't bother you for anything—"

"You don't know anything," I say, and the cold words cut through her presentation like a sword. It's the first thing I've said since she's revealed this to me, and I'm vaguely aware that my first words should have been kinder, more understanding— but how can she just stand there and announce that she's leaving like it means nothing? Like it's not going to kill me?

Like I don't love her?

And how can she think I wouldn't care that she'd be taking my baby with her?

"I know enough," she says, lifting her chin in that brash assertiveness that I love and that also drives me crazy. "I know you don't want this. I know you don't want us."

Us.

She doesn't mean me and her. She means her and the baby. *My* baby.

My blood pounds hot again, for reasons I don't entirely understand. Anger, hurt, confusion—all of those—but there's something else, something dangerous.

Possession.

"You have no idea what I want," I say, getting to my feet. She takes a step back and then another as I step forward. "You weren't even going to talk to me about this? Before you just up and left?"

Her heel hits the wall behind her and she's trapped, but she refuses to cower. "I won't ask you for anything you're not willing to give," she says proudly. "I didn't do this to trap you. I didn't do this to hurt you."

I know. It's what I should say, what I should tell her, but I'm still thrumming with this *need*, with this *fear*, that she's leaving me and I can't hold on to her, and all I want to do is hold on to her. Her and this baby.

"We can end this healthily, like adults," she says as my arms go to her waist, effectively pinning her against the wall, and her body ripples with response—goose bumps, hard nipples, parted lips.

"No," I say.

"It ended the night we met," she continues but more weakly this time.

"No," I say again, my hands dropping to her pert bottom and lifting her against me. Her legs go to my waist automatically, and she can't help the way she rubs herself against my renewed erection, just as I can't help the way I rub against her still wet and swollen pussy.

"Oliver," she tries, but my mouth is already on hers, kissing her as if I can brand my soul onto her soul, as if I can force her to stay with the heat of my lips alone.

"Red means stop," I say, and when I meet her eyes, I know the word will never leave her lips. And when I reach beneath us to aim my cock at her opening, I'm rewarded with a deep moan. This time, as I thrust into her completely naked, I savor every fucking second of it. Every tight, wet second, every inch of nothing between us.

"You were going to leave me," I grunt, pumping into her. "You were going to leave."

"It's for the best," she gasps, her arms wrapping as tight around my neck as her legs are around my waist.

I don't answer her with words, letting my mouth's actions speak for me instead, blazing hot nips and kisses down her jaw and to her neck, where I keep my face buried as I fuck her. She's so impossibly soft like this, pinned hard against a wall, not just her soft cunt but her breasts pillowing against my chest, her round bottom in my hands, and her velvet thighs around my hips. The orgasm is like a fist at the base of my spine, angry and hot, and I can feel its claws everywhere in my body, tightening in my belly and drawing up my balls and clenching the breath in my chest—but she has to go first, dammit. She's got to come first.

I drop her weight just enough so the friction catches against her clit. I feel it the moment it takes hold in her—the straining, squirming tension of her building climax—and I work it desperately, fan it into flames until she's falling into the fire of her pleasure, fluttering over the edge into release.

"Professor," she gasps, and I freeze, but she doesn't notice.

She's still riding out the waves of her orgasm on my cock, and then it doesn't matter how much the word affects me. There's no way any man can hold back now, and I am no exception. With this curvy, dark-haired goddess wet and whimpering and impaled on me, I come like a rubber band snapping, sharp and sudden and nearly painful, grunting into it like a beast.

Spurt after spurt of heat erupts into her, and it's like I can feel it everywhere, from my scalp to my toes, and I never want it to end—the feeling of pouring into her, the feeling of her still coming around me and on me and against me. And she is so perfect.

So perfect.

She deserves better than a twisted man like me.

The world slowly unwinds, slowly brings us back to normal. Normal breath, normal pulse, normal heartbeat—although my heart is still slamming wildly against my chest because I haven't just fucked Zandy the innocent little temptress. I've fucked the mother of my child.

And the responsibility of that is uncomfortably acute.

I carefully set her down and tilt her chin up to meet my face. "How are you?" I ask, abruptly worried that I fucked her too rough, that I was too much and that I've hurt her.

"I'm good," she says, a bit dazed, and then she offers me the first real smile I've seen all day. "Professor."

I flinch, just as I did when she said it a moment ago.

"What?" she asks, her forehead creasing. "What is it?"

"You can't call me that. Not—not anymore."

She keeps her eyes on me as she covers herself. "Why not?"

I'm not as brave as her, not as strong. I look away, using the fastening of my pants and shirt buttons as an excuse not to meet her eyes. "We can't play that game now."

"But I like that game." Her voice is so honest, so clear, and how does she do that? How can she make it all seem so simple? "Not just like it, Oliver, but I think I have to play it too. I need it."

"We can't do it," I repeat, sitting back down at the desk and reaching for a piece of paper. My mind is whirling, spinning, circling faster than I can keep up, as if fucking Zandy has done the opposite of settling me, it's wound me up. "That was all before, don't you see? Everything has to change now."

She goes completely still. "What do you mean?"

"I mean you're pregnant. I can't do the dirty professor routine with you, and we certainly can't keep living like this." I gesture around us to the cottage, with its gentle river noises and ordered bookshelves and sleeping cat. "I have to find a different job—a suitable one for being a father, which isn't whatever the hell I'm doing now—and we need to figure out prenatal care, first and foremost, for you, along with your visa. Ah," I say, my thoughts finally catching up to me. "We'll marry. I think we can get it done as fast as next week. That will solve a few problems fairly easily." I'm already scribbling a list of things to do, things that need to be done to keep Zandy with me, and it takes me a moment to notice that she's put her hand over the top of my paper.

I glance up at her, confused.

"You want to get married?" she asks, her voice layered with something I don't understand.

"I don't see a choice. I have a duty now—*we* have a duty now. To honor the situation."

"This isn't the Victorian ages," she says tightly. "We have more choices than we know what to do with."

But doesn't she get it? I don't want any other choices, I don't want any choice that separates me from her or from the baby. I want her.

I love her and I want her, and I can't let this end in heartbreak. I won't.

"We'll get married, and I'll stop writing and go back to teaching," I say, looking back down at the paper and adding a few more lines on the growing list of things to do.

"Okay," she says faintly, and when I finally look up later, she's left the office. Beatrix hops up on the desk and yowls at me, but I ignore her, just as I ignore the burning feeling in my chest telling me to find Zandy and hold her and tell her I love her again.

There will be time for all that later. But first, I have a duty to her and this baby, and I won't fail and I won't stop.

She'll understand.

CHAPTER FIFTEEN

ZANDY

I have to set another freak-out timer on my phone.

I give myself ten minutes this time, and I lie facedown on my bed, letting the shocked tears leak slowly out of my eyes. Did I think the worst thing that could happen was Oliver rejecting me? Did I dread him turning away in cool anger, ordering me to leave?

I've been a stupid, innocent fool, because there has always been a possibility that is much, much worse, and that is Oliver treating me like some kind of obligation. Like some kind of responsibility he has to shoulder.

I have a duty now. To honor the situation.

Oh God.

Cold rejection is so much less awful than cold acceptance. Cold duty. Talking about marrying me like it's some sort of chore, some kind of burden that has to be carried to the finish line, no matter what.

Feeling like a burden and a chore—why is that so familiar? Oh right, because it's why no one's ever wanted me before. No one's ever wanted me to date and not even to fuck, and it's probably because they could smell the *too much*ness on me.

Because they could sense I'd become a *duty* if given half the chance.

When Oliver said he loved me and then fucked me with fierce, unraveling passion against the wall, I thought—well, I didn't think. I hoped.

I hoped that all my fears and worries were misplaced and that somehow and some way, this would have a happily ever after for us. Him, me, and the baby.

But I refuse to be his cold duty. I refuse to sit around waiting for the day when his resignation becomes quiet resentment, because it will. Maybe he'll be able to keep it hidden. Maybe he'll even fool himself into accepting this new, structured life, but eventually he'll hate me for the things he's certain he has to do now.

Giving up his kink.

His research.

His freedom.

He'd hate going back to teaching and giving up on his book, and he'd hate himself for every time he wanted to get kinky with me but would feel like he couldn't. And he'd hate me for marrying him and invading his quiet bubble of a life. I don't know why he thinks he has to give all that up because I'm pregnant, but I know him well enough to tell he won't be moved.

Which only means one thing. It's up to me.

By the time my timer goes off, I've dried my tears and started packing. And by the time Oliver notices I'm missing, it will be far too late.

♦ ♦ ♦ ♦

Two Days Later...

My father's voice is echoing off the kitchen tile in a dry rumble that used to put me to sleep every night as he read to me when I was a child. The familiar sound of it makes me want to cry, but I can't tell if that's lingering jet lag or the baby hormones.

"Yes, she's here," I hear him say, and then there's a long pause. "She's sleeping now. But I can tell her you've called. Again."

I bury my face in my pillow, wishing my bedroom weren't just right up the stairs from the kitchen. Wishing I didn't have to hear the phone ring over and over again with Oliver trying to talk to me.

In a flash of masochism, I lift up my own phone to peek at the screen. Tens, if not hundreds, of notifications, emails, texts, phone calls, everything—all from Oliver.

All from my terrifyingly sexy professor.

It was awful sneaking out of the cottage—more than awful. I thought I was dying as I climbed into the cab waiting outside, as Beatrix sat perched on the stone bench inside the front garden and tilted her little cat head at me. I hated leaving. I hated walking away from the cottage, with its blown flowers and leafy vines and old stone walls. I hated hearing the river nearby, shallow and bright, knowing I'd never hear it again. And I even hated poor little Beatrix for making me love her when she should have known better.

I hated leaving Oliver.

I hated knowing that his polished voice and mysterious eyes wouldn't be mine to hear and to see any longer. I hated how hard it was to sneak away because I also hated how impossible it would be to say goodbye. I would try to leave, and he'd be too handsome, too smart, too magnetic, and I'd stay anyway, even though my staying would wreck his life and ultimately make him loathe me for the part I played in wrecking it.

No, this was the way it was always going to be.

And I hated that most of all.

It only took Oliver an hour or so to realize I was gone, but an hour was all I needed. I was most of the way to Birmingham by then, and I made my way through security and to a flight before he could reach me. Then, like with all the calls and emails today, he was acting out of duty, and I bet even now the relief is starting to creep in. The relief that I won't be ruining his life after all.

I don't read the emails or the texts. I don't let myself. Because as much as I want Oliver to be feeling relief right now, as much as I want to think I've found a way to walk out of this with my head held high, I feel nothing but agony.

Maybe there's a tiny part of me that hopes he'll board a plane to America. That he'll come chasing after me.

It's ridiculous and childish—sheer nonsense given what I've done and how I've refused to talk to him—but maybe I'm too Zandy Lynch *not* to be ridiculous and childish sometimes. Yet another reason Oliver and I would never have worked.

My father appears in my doorway, holding out a mug of coffee for me, which I take even though I won't drink it. I haven't told him about the pregnancy yet—or even that Oliver and I were briefly a thing—although I think he's pieced that together from my unexpected arrival home and Oliver's many phone calls.

"Do you want me to take you to your apartment?" Dad asks softly. "At least to get some fresh clothes?"

I look down at my flannel unicorn pajamas—a relic from my high school years that I found in my old dresser. "I guess I should. But...can I stay here for a few more days?"

He softens, trundling over and sitting on the edge of my bed. "You know I'm always happy to have you here, Zandy. No matter what's going on."

He takes my hand, and I try not to cry in earnest. My dad has always been like this—loyal and quiet and easy. God, how I wish I'd been born the same! Instead of messy and loud and *too much*.

"Dad? Were you ever scared about having me?"

He looks down at my face, and understanding rearranges the smile on his face into something both kinder and sadder.

He knows.

Maybe it's my question or his fatherly intuition, but it's plain that he's just figured it out, and he squeezes my hand.

"When I found out your mother was pregnant, I felt nothing but excitement, because I knew I could do anything with that amazing woman at my side. But when she died..." His eyes grow glassy, and I know he's seeing memories I'm too young to remember. Memories of hospital beds and doctor visits. "I was more than scared. I was paralyzed. Because I didn't think I could do it without her. You were six then and still so young, and every good part of you was because of her.

What if I ruined you somehow? What if I stifled all the parts of you that had only flowered because of your mother?"

He's never told me this before, and I sit up a little, curious. "What do you mean, because of her?"

Dad smiles fondly. "I've told you how smart and driven she was, but have I ever told you how funny and friendly she was? How determined? How brave? She could march into a room full of strangers and have them loving her within minutes. She could travel to a country she'd never been to, and within a day, she was already learning the language and having adventures. She was the opposite of me and perfect in every way. And when I saw how like her you were...I wanted to treasure that at all costs. I still do."

I give him a hug, overcome, swelling with pain and pride. "I never knew," I whisper, my eyes leaking tears onto his shoulder.

"I should have told you. But it's hard to talk about for me, and for you...for you, I only wanted you to look forward to your future. Not be stuck with me in a painful past."

"But what do I do now?" I ask tearfully. "What comes next?"

"That, my brave girl, only you can answer. But I will say that I believe fear is part of the process. It's what makes the joy all the more precious in the end."

"That's very wise," I say, sniffling as I pull back.

"Go easy on Oliver," Dad says gently. "Men like us sometimes need longer to become as brave as you and your mom were. He'll find his way."

I shake my head. "He was willing to do so much for me,

but it felt all wrong. It felt like he was forcing himself, and I decided at the beginning of the summer that I wouldn't be that girl. That clingy girl who grabbed on to any promise of a future, no matter how emotionally coerced it was."

"So noble," Dad says. "But did you ever consider it's the other way around? That he's trying to cling on to you and just doesn't know how?"

I frown. "It didn't feel like that."

"He's lost someone before, and it sounds to me like the first thing he wanted to make sure of was that he didn't lose you too. Think about it, pumpkin." And with that, Dad drops a kiss on my forehead and leaves me to my thoughts.

Could he be right?

Was Oliver trying to hold on to me, as opposed to grimly shouldering me like some kind of burden?

Did he...*want* me?

And the baby?

And even if he did, would he ever forgive me for running away?

CHAPTER SIXTEEN

OLIVER

I thought I already lived through the worst day of my life. I thought what happened with Rosie was the worst thing I would ever go through, but as I walk through the house calling Zandy's name and realizing with cold, encroaching horror that she is gone, I know I was wrong.

This is the worst day of my life.

This is having my heart broken.

And the shitty thing? I absolutely know why. I know I deserve it.

I walk back into the study where I had her pinned to the wall not an hour before, where I held her curled and crying in my lap.

God, what a fuckup I am. I should have held her until night fell. I should have dropped to my knees and worshiped her. I should have cradled her and murmured how happy I was, how much I loved her, how I would take care of her as long as she'd let me. I should have been honest. I should have just *talked*.

But my God, how could she have expected me to respond right away? Wasn't a man allowed some time to process news like this?

Even as I think a bitter *apparently not,* raking my hand through my hair, I know it doesn't matter. I didn't even *ask* her to marry me, I just told her that we'd do it—God, no wonder she left. I fucked up. Something that becomes more and more apparent as she refuses to answer my calls.

Shit. Where could she have gone? Where does she have to go? I'm the only person she knows here. My cottage is the only place she has that's not in America—

Oh fuck.

The flight from Birmingham. Of course, she even told me about it, but somehow I wasn't able to connect that with her absence now, because, pathetically, I suppose I've been holding out hope that she wouldn't do something so drastic, so...real.

What else is she supposed to do? Stay in a country that's not her own while she carries the child of a man who was grimly planning an emergency wedding?

Good God, I've become my own Victorian morality narrative.

Fuck.

I get in my car and speed to the airport, but I know even as I wince my way through all the speed traps that I'll be too late. Zandy doesn't do anything by half-measures, and she has a plan for everything—whether it's arranging my hallway bookshelves or getting Beatrix to switch to dry cat food. There's no way in hell she doesn't have a concrete plan for escape. She made a spreadsheet to help her decide what to do about this pregnancy, for pity's sake.

And even as I fruitlessly search the public parts of the

airport, I can't help but admire her. Even her spreadsheets and escape routes. Even her spine of steel normally hidden behind schoolgirl enthusiasm and lush curves.

How could I have been so foolish as to let a woman like her slip through my fingers?

◆ ◆ ◆ ◆

"Zandy, thank fuck."

I'm in my study, warm summer darkness pressing up against the windows and Beatrix lying sideways on my desk, watching me pace the floor. A floor I can only pace because of Zandy's hard work in organizing my research.

"Oliver," Zandy says quietly. I know it's morning in the States—in the last three days of ceaselessly calling and emailing, I've become something of an expert in time zones—but she sounds exhausted. Raspy, like she's been crying.

The thought of it burns in my chest.

"I just—" I stop, searching for the right words to say. I'm still stunned she finally picked up the phone, and I don't want to say anything wrong. I don't want to scare her away. "How are you? And the baby?"

"The baby is currently the size of a pomegranate seed," Zandy says. "So I think it's fine."

She doesn't answer how she is, and she doesn't have to. Her voice says it all.

"Zandy, I—I fucked up. I should have listened. I should have talked. I should have done everything differently."

There's silence on the other end, and somehow I know it wasn't good enough, that she needs more. "I love you," I say.

Plead. "I want you. And this baby. And I'll do anything to prove it."

"Are those the things you think you have to say?" she asks softly. Too softly, but I don't see the danger.

"Of course. Aren't they the things you need to hear?"

A sharp breath, like a gasp. From all the way across the Atlantic, it sounds like a gunshot.

"Zandy? What did I say wrong? Tell me, *tell me* and I'll fix it, I swear to God."

"Don't you see?" she whispers. "I don't want this to be about what you think you should do. I don't want you to leave your research. I don't want you to marry me if you are only doing it out of some kind of half-baked obligation of honor."

I sputter a little at that, but she's not done.

"And I especially don't want you to give up the professor games. How could I, when they make me feel more alive than I've ever felt? When they're a part of *you*, and I love every part of you?"

The burning in my chest is a fire now, an inferno, and it's searing my very soul. "I love you too, Zandy. Don't you see that's why I'm willing to give up anything to be with you?"

"And don't you see that's why I can't let you?" Her voice wavers, and I know she's close to tears, if she's not already crying. Damn this distance, this ocean! I tighten my hand around my phone as if I can pull her back to me through the tiny device.

"I want you just as you are," she continues. "And I refuse to be the reason you ruin your life. I'm sorry that Rosie made you feel like you didn't deserve a child or a future because of the things you like in bed, but dammit, Oliver, if you can't see how absurd that is after all these years, then I don't know how to make you."

Defensiveness wells up in my throat. "It's not absurd. It's reality. People like me can't have families; that's why I have to change."

"But money isn't an issue, so you shouldn't need to change jobs, and there's no law that says we have to be married to have a child together. And there's certainly no law that says people can't have playful sex after they have a baby. You're inventing this new version of yourself that's wholly unnecessary, and it's a new version I don't want. I love you how you are, and I refuse to be the excuse for you to hurt yourself." She takes a deep breath, and it trembles enough that I know she's truly crying now. "I love you, but I deserve more than being a duty. I deserve the man I love—*as he is*—choosing me because he's happy to choose me. Not because he feels forced."

She hangs up, and the sudden silence on the other end might kill me, save for one thing.

I understand now.

She isn't upset that I hadn't acted happy enough. She wants to save me from the mire of self-loathing I've been in since Rosie left me. And for the first time in years, I not only want to save myself, but I recognize that I don't have to. I didn't love Rosie in any real measure, and I've been a fool to let her words fester and slowly infect me.

If Zandy will have me as a crabby scholar who delights in taking her over my knee, then that's what she will get.

And to hell with the rest.

CHAPTER SEVENTEEN

ZANDY

Whoosh-whoosh-whoosh-whoosh-whoosh.

I blink at the screen next to me. Everything just looks like a swirl of static, except for the tiny spot at the middle. "Is that sound the heartbeat?" I whisper.

The ultrasound tech smiles at me. "It is. Baby's doing just fine."

I let out a long breath of relief. In the handful of days since Oliver's phone call, I've had light, persistent cramping—nothing too scary, but my new nurse-midwife wanted to make sure everything was progressing well all the same.

I stare at the little bean on the ultrasound monitor, as if it will make the storming thoughts inside my head clearer. As if it will loosen the painful knot in my chest.

It doesn't, but I still feel a spike of mind-boggling awe—as well as a spike of regret. Oliver should be here right now. Oliver should be here to see his child. Even if there's no future for us, he deserves that much at least.

"I'm going to run these images over to your midwife and make sure she doesn't want anything else," the ultrasound tech says, snapping her gloves off and taking some printouts away from the machine. "Stay here."

As if I'm going anywhere naked below the waist and still slicked up with the bluish lube they used for the ultrasound wand. I consider reaching for my phone as the door closes behind the tech, but I decide against it. I'll only be crushed by how blank it is; Oliver hasn't tried to call or contact me at all since we last spoke on the phone.

I close my eyes against the sudden burn, feeling stupid. This is what I wanted, right? Dignity, distance, all of the stuff that sounds so good in theory and *Cosmo* articles.

In real life, however, dignity sucks.

My eyes are still closed as the tech comes back in the room, and I take a deep breath, preparing to act the part of chipper young mom again. It's been a little embarrassing, being here alone, knowing the front desk girls and the clucking, brusque nurses are all forming their own opinions about me, but it's nothing I can't handle, right?

Right.

But before I can open my eyes to greet the tech again, I feel a blunt finger tracing the narrow leather band of my wristwatch. "Always this watch," a wry British voice says. "Even now."

I open my eyes.

He'll never stop being so fucking handsome, will he? The unkempt shadow of a beard on that square jaw matches his tousled hair perfectly, and even the sleepless smudges under his eyes only serve to set off the unfairly long eyelashes and the hypnotically colored eyes. That sensual mouth is currently twisted in a smile so aristocratically and perfectly Oliver

Markham Graeme that I could cry.

"You're here," I say pointlessly.

He settles a hand over my lower stomach, but his eyes never leave my face. "I'm here," he affirms.

"But..." I don't have the rest of the words to finish my objection, although it's not really an objection. Even with everything between us, seeing him is like swallowing down pure excitement. A hot flush of happiness starts to creep up my cheeks.

He notices, his smile becoming less dry and more tender. He brushes along my blush-stained cheeks with the back of a finger. "But nothing, darling. You were right. About everything."

"Everything?" I ask, suddenly finding myself uncertain in the trance of his beautiful eyes.

"I wish you hadn't left," he admits. "I wish you would have told me about the baby the moment you found out...but I understand why you didn't. It took you calling me absurd before the truth became clear to me."

"I didn't call *you* absurd," I clarify quickly. "Just your weird self-loathing."

He laughs, the act transforming his expression into that boyish, happy face I love so much. "Okay, fine then. It took you calling my self-loathing absurd for me to understand." He sobers a little, his hand splaying so nice and warm on my belly. "And I think I do understand now. I never wanted you to feel like a duty, Zandy. I want you because I want you. And if you'll have me the way I am"—his eyes meet mine—"then I'm all yours."

I search his expression. "So you aren't going to insist on marriage?"

"I want to marry you, but only if you're willing." The look on his face is fierce and loving. "And I'll be there as long as it takes to make you willing."

"And you're not going to quit your writing and go take a teaching job you hate?"

"No."

"And you'll still be a spanky professor with me?"

He rolls his eyes at the word *spanky*, but a smile tugs at his lips. "And I'll still be a spanky professor with you."

I finally allow myself to grin. "Then that's all I can ask for."

The tech opens the door, making a coo of surprise when she sees Oliver. "Is this Daddy?" she asks, bustling back to the machine.

"Yes," Oliver and I say at the same time.

And we manage to sway the tech into showing us a few more minutes of the baby, even though technically she doesn't need to, and I soak in every moment of Oliver's reserved expression made open and awed with wonder as he watches his baby's heart pulse on the screen.

It's not until we're leaving the office together, several glossy prints of our baby in hand, when I nudge his arm with my shoulder and say, "You're Daddy now."

His gorgeous mouth hooks up at the corner. "Sometimes I'll be, Miss Lynch. But when we're alone, I'm still Professor."

I think I might float away with happiness. "Yes, sir," I say, and I'm rewarded with a kiss that steals my breath right out of my mouth and promises all sorts of dirty, spanky things to come.

As long as I'm a very, very good girl.

EPILOGUE

OLIVER

One Year Later...

Warm summer air blows through the study windows, ruffling my papers. I mumble a frustrated oath, clapping a hand over the pile and trying to ignore Zandy, who is finishing up her assignment using completely digitized materials and is visibly smug about it. Ever since she decided to go to library school in nearby Sheffield, we've been sharing my study, and she's never stopped fussing about my affinity for paper. Or rather, the way the paper I work with tends to clump into piles and stacks and turn our neatly organized study into a warren of discarded books.

The breeze blows again, toying with her hair and fluttering the edges of her blouse, drawing my eyes down to her chest. The baby and nursing have blown out Zandy's buxom shape, transforming her girlishly curvy body to something ripe and irresistible. Looking at her now makes me feel distinctly barbarian-like; I can't catch sight of those lush, milk-heavy breasts or those suggestively wide hips without wanting to throw her over my shoulder and carry her off to some remote tower and mate with her until we both can't move anymore.

I consider doing that right now—sans tower, of course—when a small squeak draws my attention. I look over to the small cot next to my desk, where two chubby waving fists and slowly kicking legs alert me that my little man is awake.

Zandy starts to stand, but I beat her to him, scooping up the squishy bug in my arms and kissing his thick, silky crown of hair. At three months old, Michael—named for her father—looks almost all my child: his eyes so blue at birth now changing into speckles of green and brown as well, his pointed chin, and even his little frowns and scowls. But the hair is all from his mother, and I find myself so fucking enamored sometimes with the idea that he's been created uniquely and solely from me and the woman I love.

The woman who's going to be my wife.

After our conversation and my botched attempt at marrying her the first time, I decided to take no risks with my second approach, and in a very Zandy-ish move, I made a plan. Part of the plan was establishing where we would live and where she would go to school, because I can live anywhere, really, and I knew she'd want to be close to her father. I let her choose every step of the way, reminding her that I'd love her and stay with her no matter what.

She chose England and the cottage and the river and then began a campaign of emotional warfare to convince her father to find a job here near us. A campaign that was successful. He lives a mere ten minutes away from his grandson now.

The other part of the plan was to simply enjoy the process of having Michael. I didn't want to rush her or pressure her when she seemed so happy and alight with his impending arrival, so I decided to wait until after his birth to settle this once and for all.

Zandy's mine.

She's been mine from the moment I covered my body with hers and slid inside her. Hell, she's been mine since the moment she stumbled into me on a rainy London night.

And I have no intention of letting her go.

Zandy finishes up her work while I tend to Michael, and by the time she's finished, he's ready to nurse. I sit at the edge of my desk and watch as she props her feet up on a pile of books and cradles our son to her breast.

I watch appreciatively, happily, because she's a vision like this—her hair in tumble-down waves over her shoulders and her beautiful face bent in tender care...and her perfect breast available to view. As if hearing my thoughts, my son puts a flexing hand over her breast as if to lay claim.

I smile, dropping a kiss on his head as I get up to prepare for this afternoon. *Message received, little sir*, I think with amusement. *She's all yours for now*.

But after he nods off into his habitual milk coma and we lay him down in his nursery upstairs, I lead Zandy back to the study, because for the next hour, she's all mine. And I intend on using that time very well.

The moment I sit back down at my desk and say, "Come here, Miss Lynch," my cock swells against my trousers in Pavlovian response. And it swells even more as I see the rampant evidence of her desire stamped all over her body—nipples like hard little bullets, cheeks stained pink, and her even, white teeth biting into her lower lip.

"Yes, Professor," she murmurs, coming toward me with a smile she can't quite hide.

"I'm afraid you've been a bad girl," I tell her sternly, "and the time has come to do something about it."

"I haven't been a bad girl," she protests as she finally reaches me, and I hear the real umbrage in her voice—my Zandy is someone who always wants to be a good girl, the teacher's pet, and even though she knows it's a game, she still can't stifle the eager schoolgirl inside her who wants to please me entirely. Her puzzled little frown is only half-faked. "I'm a good girl, I promise."

"I don't think so," I say, giving her the steely teacher-ish glare that makes her melt every time. "We need to have a talk about your behavior, Miss Lynch. And about the consequences."

I stand up, and her teeth sink back into her lip in a display of contrition. Heat pools at the base of my spine, and I have to consciously control my breathing and slow it down. *Fuck*, how I need this game. How I need *her* to play it with. Only her, for the rest of my life.

"Do you think I haven't noticed what you've been doing to get my attention, Miss Lynch? The staying after class? The 'extra studying' in my office? And do you think I haven't noticed how you shamelessly display your body to me?"

Deep blue eyes peer up at me through dark, fluttering lashes. "I wasn't doing it on purpose," she breathes. "I promise, sir."

I slide my hand into the loose, silky hair at the nape of her neck. "I think it was on purpose," I say coldly. "I think you are deliberately trying to provoke me. And I think you're about to learn how far you can provoke a man before he acts."

"Acts?" she asks, blinking up at me.

I yank her close enough that she can feel the hot column of my cock against her belly. "That's right, Miss Lynch. It's time for you to face the consequences of your misbehavior."

And then I bend her over the desk.

I'm trembling. I'm almost always trembling by this point, the sheer fucking filthiness of it throbbing deep in my belly and shuddering heat all the way to the tip of my leaking cock. Something about this game rocks me to my core, makes me feel like every time is the first time, and the fact that I can play it with someone who loves it as much as I do is incredible. I'm humbled by it every single fucking time.

She looks up at me over her shoulder, delivering her most innocent pout. "But sir, I won't be bad any longer. I'll be good, I swear."

I flip up her skirt, exposing a round behind and a sweet pussy that are completely bare. No underthings at all. "This doesn't look like you have any plans to be good anytime soon," I say darkly, giving her pussy a hard cup. "I think you're lying. I think you can't help yourself, and you're going to keep this pussy wet and open for me whenever I'm around because you can't stand not having me fuck you, hmm?"

She grinds down against my hand, chasing the pressure and rolling her head along her folded forearms.

"Answer me, girl. Are you going to start behaving now?" I time my question with the dirty, probing slide of one finger deep into her heat, and she mewls at me.

"No, Professor, I'm so sorry. I just can't help it..."

"Then you'll have to face the consequences of your behavior," I say, injecting my voice with as much grimness as I can muster through all the lust currently pounding through my veins. "How do you stop me, Miss Lynch?"

"Red," she moans, whimpering in protest as I remove my finger. "But please don't ever stop."

Thwack.

The first stinging slap across her ass makes her jolt against the desk, one of her bare little feet kicking up reflexively. I move my own feet around hers, enjoying the picture we make very much—the trouser fabric against bare legs and the rumpled plaid waves of her skirt, the expensive leather of my shoes against the adorable red-painted toes and pale skin of her feet. I give her another quick slap and then sit back down in my chair.

"Over my knee, Miss Lynch. I need to make sure you're not getting too comfortable."

The look she cuts me is a prism of all the things I love about our game, about our life. It's fear and arousal and the distinct slice of rueful affection, and it hardens my cock at the same time it softens my heart. I love her, and I love the way we fit together as I pull her over my lap, as she drops a soft kiss on my forearm, and as I give her thigh a quick, reassuring squeeze before we disappear back into the game.

I pull her skirt up to her waist and spank her until she squirms. I spank her until her legs start kicking up and I have to trap them under my leg to keep punishing her. I keep it nice today, my palm working over a liberal area and striking just hard enough to burn but not hard enough to truly hurt. And then once she's nice and pink, I part her legs to inspect her pussy.

"Wet," I declare harshly. "Shamefully wet. I don't think you've learned your lesson at all."

"Maybe not," she gasps as my inspecting hand starts rubbing at her cunt. "I might need more punishment."

"A shame," I say, picking her up and bending her back over the desk. With one hand, I keep her bent over the desk while my other hand fumbles with my trousers to release my aching erection. "I had such hopes I could turn you back into a good girl."

"I can be a good girl starting right now," she begs, lifting up on her tiptoes and bringing her wet, flushed opening level with my cock. I rub my tip against it, enjoying the heat and the slick kiss of her flesh against mine, enjoying her needy moans even more. And finally, finally, after shoving the turgid head into the small seam and lodging myself there, I thrust home.

She's so tight, so hot, that static fuzzes at the edges of my vision. "I've changed my mind," I say breathlessly. "You are a very good girl. Utterly perfect."

She tosses her hair over her shoulder as she sends me the kind of saucy look no actual good girl could ever muster. "I like it when you fuck me, Professor," she says, and she pushes back against me to prove her point. "You make me feel so good."

I give her a stinging spank and then reach in front of her to add my fingers to her pleasure, knowing how she likes the pressure of my touch on her clit as I fuck her tight opening from behind. And it doesn't take her long like this, with me riding her against the desk and my touch on her intimate secrets, and she comes with a surprised wail, clenching so hard around my cock that I very nearly lose it.

But I cling on, by fingernails and teeth, desperate to execute my plan. Because one thing's become clear to me over the past year, and it's how much we need each other like this and how afraid Zandy was of losing this part of me. So I need to prove to her now that she'll never lose it, that it's part of our love now and forever.

After her peak subsides, I reach over and slide a piece of notebook paper in front of her. "I forgot to mention this very important assignment," I say, and I see her glance at it briefly and then back to me, as if she expects it only to have the usual *red means stop* scrawled across, since that's usually how I check in with her during our games.

But this time it says something different.

I see the moment she realizes this, the moment her head dips back to read the paper again, and she freezes underneath my now-leisurely stroking hips.

I love you, the paper says. *Will you marry me? Will you be my wife and let me be your professor?*

"Oliver," she says, and her voice is filled with tears.

I pull out enough that I can turn her around and guide her back onto the desk, on her back this time, and I crawl over her, entering her with a wet, welcome shove.

"I love you. And I want you as you are," I murmur into her mouth, punctuating my words with deep, stroking kisses. "Will you have me? Just as I am?"

"Yes," she says, her tears running off her smiling cheeks. "Yes, I want you. Yes, I'll have you."

"So it's settled, then," I say, feeling like I've swallowed sunshine and grinning like an idiot. "You're mine."

She gives me a challenging look. "And you're mine too."

"Just so."

And when we come together, hot and messy and slick on top of my desk, surrounded by the library she built and with our baby sleeping upstairs, it's not the beginning of something incredible—the beginning happened on a drenching night over a year ago. But it's a confirmation.

A confirmation and a conclusion, and for me being the professor, I have to admit the woman underneath me has taught me more than I ever could have imagined. I couldn't have planned the lesson better myself, although as we start kissing and grinding our way to a second round, I decide there's no way I can ever admit that to her.

I am the professor in this house, after all.

EXCERPT FROM
MISADVENTURES ON THE REBOUND

The sexy dude entering the bar looks to be in his mid-twenties. He's holding a motorcycle helmet in one hand and a dark backpack in the other. He's got sandy hair, a chiseled jaw, and light eyes framed by bold eyebrows. His extremely fit body is clothed in a dark leather jacket, worn jeans, and a blue T-shirt that matches his stunning eyes. In short, he's perfect.

My heart thumping, I turn back around and take a long gulp of my drink and, a few seconds later, Mr. Perfect bellies up to the bar to my right.

The air between us fills with the delicious scents of him: leather, faint aftershave, and the great outdoors. He places his helmet atop the bar and his backpack on the ground and greets the bartender in a low, masculine voice. "Hey, man."

"What'll it be?" Cal replies, placing a cocktail napkin in front of the guy.

"Whatever will get me shitfaced and stupid in short order," comes Mr. Perfect's perfect reply.

"Great minds think alike," I murmur.

"Huh?"

I clear my throat. Under normal circumstances, I wouldn't initiate contact with a stranger in a bar, especially not a stranger who looks like this guy. But, today, normal rules don't apply, apparently. Today, I'm all out of fucks to give. "I said, 'Great minds think alike.' Meaning my plan is to get shitfaced and stupid in short order, too." I raise my drink. "Indeed, I'm well on my way. This is my second drink, and I'm a lightweight, especially after eight months of not drinking."

"Well, damn. As long as we're both getting shitfaced and stupid tonight, we should probably do it together, don't you think? Drinking is a lot like sex. You can do it alone, but it's a whole lot more fun with a partner."

I can't help returning his wicked smile. I motion to the stool next to me. "Please."

"Thanks." He settles himself and the delicious scents attached to him intensify. "So what are you drinking?" he asks.

"Whiskey sours," I say. "But, actually, I'm imbibing, not drinking. Because drinking is sad." I make a sad face. "But imbibing is *fun*." I make a happy face that makes him chuckle. "Actually, no, that was a lie," I say. "I'm not imbibing. I'm most definitely drinking. Drowning my sorrows, in fact. I've had a horribly shitty day, and I'm numbing the pain."

"Sorry to hear that. Is the whiskey doing the trick?"

I slap my face. "So far, so good."

"Perfect." He motions to Cal. "I'll have whatever the fuck this gorgeous woman is having. And add her drinks to my tab. A woman this beautiful, especially one having a horribly shitty day, can't pay for her own drinks. Not on my watch, anyway."

Every cell in my body spazzes out, all at once. "Thank you," I say, my cheeks blooming. "I appreciate it."

"My pleasure." He leans toward me. "I'm not doing it simply to be nice. I'm trying to seduce you after having a horribly shitty day myself."

"*Oh*. Wow. Thanks for letting me know."

He winks. "Sure thing."

The bartender slides a drink in front of Mr. Perfect, and he raises it to me. "Cheers," he says. "To getting shitfaced and stupid and numbing the pain."

"Cheers to that." I clink his glass. "Although I hope you're not planning to get *too* shitfaced and stupid. I'm quite certain Uber doesn't pick up out here in 1982, and I'd hate to see that thing turn into a brain bucket on you." I motion to his helmet on the bar.

"Thanks for your concern, but I won't be driving anywhere tonight, unfortunately. Hence, my horribly shitty day. My bike crapped out on me a couple miles back, and I had to push it until I came upon the garage across the street. As it turns out, they had to order a part, which means I'm stranded for at least a couple days."

I grimace sympathetically.

"And that was just the tip of the iceberg of my horribly shitty day," he adds. He exhales. "So I've decided to get shitfaced and stupid, crash at the motel tonight, and figure out my game plan tomorrow morning."

"Great minds think alike again," I say. "That's my exact

itinerary, as well. I've already booked my room at the motel."

"You're one step ahead of me there. I came straight to this bar after the garage. But don't worry about me. I promise I'll be crashing at the motel tonight." He flashes me a wicked smile and winks. "One way or another."

Holy crap. Did this sexy man just call his shot? Did he just imply he'll be sleeping with me in *my* room tonight? By George, I think he did. "So where were you headed when your bike broke down?" I ask.

"Vegas. What about you? Unless, of course, this place was your final destination."

"No, I stumbled upon this place by chance. I'm actually headed to Vegas, too. I grew up there, and my five-year high school reunion is this Saturday night."

I wait. Surely, he's going to try to bum a ride to Vegas from me now. And what will I say? It'd be no inconvenience for me to take him. And I'd thoroughly enjoy glancing over at him for three solid hours during the drive. And yet, on the other hand, I think I've seen this particular after-school special...and it didn't end well for the female driver who picked up a handsome stranger.

But, nope. Much to my surprise, he doesn't broach the subject. Instead, he takes a long sip of his drink and mutters, "If that's your second drink, then I've got some catching up to do."

I return his smirk. "If you want to keep up with me, then you'd better make your next drink a double." I throw back the rest of my drink and place my empty onto the bar next to his. "I'm not fucking around today. I'm done fucking around."

His eyes blaze. "Damn." He chuckles. "I hope you don't mind me saying this, but that was sexy as fuck."

I grin. "I don't mind you saying it at all."

"Good. Because it was." He motions to the bartender. "Hey, Cal. Another round. And on the recommendation of this sexy-as-fuck woman, you'd better make mine a double."

I can't breathe. My heart is medically palpitating. This is the most electrifying interaction with a man I've ever had in my life. I lean into his broad shoulder. "I hope you don't mind me saying this, but I think you're sexy as fuck, too."

"I don't mind you saying that at all. In fact, I'm thrilled to know the attraction is mutual." He sticks out his hand. "I'm Aiden, by the way. Nice to meet you."

I take his hand, and electricity zings and zaps across my flesh at the point of contact. "Savvy," I say. "But don't let the name fool you."

Aiden cocks his head to the side. "So does that mean your name is Savvy, but you're not *savvy*?"

I giggle. "Correct. My full name is Savannah. Savannah Valentine. But I've always been called Savvy. And that's just a ridiculous nickname for me because I'm the least savvy person you'll ever meet. I've got book smarts for days. But street smarts? Not so much."

"Sounds like we're a perfect match. I've got *street* smarts for days, but book smarts? Not so much."

"Wow. I'd totally pick you for my zombie apocalypse team, Aiden."

"I'm honored. Thanks. And I'd pick you."

"Thank you."

Aiden chuckles and leans his forearms on the bar. "So, tell me, Savvy Who Isn't Savvy, why's a smart, funny, pretty girl like you sitting in a bar in the middle of nowhere on a Wednesday afternoon, drowning your sorrows?"

Surprised, I look down at my ruby ring, my cheeks flushing.

Aiden adds quickly, "Unless, of course, you don't feel comfortable talking about it."

I look up. Aiden's eyes are warm and comforting and gorgeously blue. He's truly magnificent to behold. "No, I...I actually *want* to babble about what happened today. You just surprised me, that's all. The way you looked so genuinely interested and...compassionate."

He smiles and my heart flutters.

"Do you want the short or long version of my story?"

"Long, of course. I've got nowhere to go, remember? Tell me everything."

This story continues in
Misadventures on the Rebound!

ACKNOWLEDGMENTS

Firstly, thanks go to my beautiful and tireless agent, Rebecca Friedman, whose confidence in my writing is unwavering (and probably undeserved, but I'm taking it anyway!).

To my editor, Scott Saunders, for his sharp eye and flawless observations, and to the rest of the Waterhouse team: Meredith Wild, Robyn Lee, Jennifer Becker, David Grishman, Yvonne Ellis, Haley Byrd, Kurt Vachon, Jonathan Mac, and Jesse Kench. And my undying thanks to Amber Maxwell for a staggeringly good cover!

To Ashley Lindemann, Serena McDonald, Candi Kane, and Melissa Gaston for their help and support with all the back-of-the-house work that comes along with writing a book. To Laurelin Paige, Melanie Harlow, and Kayti McGee, as well as Julie Murphy, Natalie Parker, Tess Gratton, Nana Malone, Sarah MacLean, Carrie Ryan, Jana Aston, and Becca Mysoor—along with everyone else at the Orange Beach and Kiawah retreats for all the support and laughter (and occasionally liquor). And huge and grateful thanks to Karen Cundy, who made sure Oliver sounded more Cambridge than Kansas.

To Doug Hagen, Eddy Bisceglia, Dana Hagen, Kay Hagen, Sandra Whitman, Ed Wells, Lizzie Hagen, and

Kathie and Milt Taylor for supporting the brooding author in their lives. And to Josh Taylor, who has to support her most of all.

And lastly to my readers. Thank you for going on yet another dirty, fun journey with me!

MORE MISADVENTURES

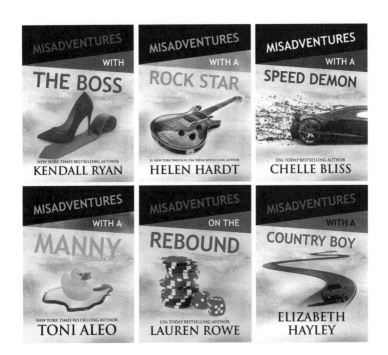

VISIT MISADVENTURES.COM
FOR MORE INFORMATION!